Shooting Albatrosses

Shooting Albatrosses

Leon Paulin

ISBN 978-0-473-34492-4

Cover design and layout DIY Publishing Ltd

Dedication

For Sylvia, without whom
this book would not have been written.

And for Sophia and Suzie.

Acknowledgements

I would like to thank Jim Parsons for his experience, support and encouragement in the writing of this book. And it was always a great privilege to have such open access to his 'built-in bullshit detector.'

Contents

ONE

MATT SQUIRMED on the couch as he toyed with the envelope. This wasn't just any old letter; it held his economics exam results, which he had already read online. His father snatched it from him, used his forefinger to break the seal and extracted the results. On unfolding the paper, his mouth dropped, and his face went the colour of beetroot out of the can.

"What's … this?" His father tried to go on but nothing came.

Matt's mother peered over his shoulder.

"Isn't it obvious?" Matt stood to his full height and picked at his thumbnail. His brown hair curled to his ears and his eyes blazed blue. He leaned over them, legs apart.

The Saturday morning sun shone low into the open plan living area and made him squint. The constant need to meet his father's standards always made him anxious. For now he wanted to enjoy the summer holidays, not think about a career. From his position he could see the beach traffic, walkers wrapped in towels, and cars with surfboards on top. A cool, onshore wind wafted through the open window.

"I'm disappointed," his father said. "Pretty average results." His mouth hardened into a flat line.

Matt knew average was a dirty word to his father. He watched him shift position on the couch, draping one leg over the other and smoothing his grey trousers. He always looked immaculate.

Matt's mother sat beside him in a crumpled pink leisure suit, her hazel eyes alert and intense as she peered around his father to watch the news on TV.

"Let him be," she said, and wriggled in her seat.

"I have been, and look where it's got us." His father fidgeted with his cellphone.

It seemed to Matt his father was on edge today and the poor grades had made him worse. This is how it always seemed lately. If only he could make his escape to the beach, the one place where all his problems seem to melt into the air. He wished he was surfing. "I want a bit of fun," he said, as he watched President Obama step out of Air Force One on the TV.

The door knocker thunked. Matt opened the door to his mate BJ, who wore cargo shorts and a Hawaiian shirt with a baseball cap on backwards like some sort of American hip-hop tourist. He had a girl with him.

"Hi, I'm Kristy," she said to everybody.

"I know," Matt said. "I've seen you round school."

Kristy wore pink shorts and a lavender tank top.

"Nice to meet you, Kristy," Matt's mother and father said simultaneously.

Matt caught a big whiff of Kristy's perfume; it drowned out the salt air. It smelled of spring flowers, and she looked beautiful in a beach girl studenty sort of way. He wondered how BJ managed to be friends with such a hot girl; they were a very odd couple.

"Come on," Matt said, "grab a seat," and he flipped his hand towards the two-seater couch, which faced the room and backed to the window that had a view of the road.

His mother talked at them from across the room. "You must tell us about yourself, Kristy. What did you say your last name was?"

"Jamieson," she said, turning red in the face.

"I know a lawyer by that name." Matt's father beamed.

"Yes, that's my dad," Kristy replied.

BJ quickly changed the subject. "Kristy's in my drama club." He twirled his cap to the front as he spoke.

"Yes," Kristy said, "BJ's going to teach me to surf." She looked at BJ and her sweetheart lips parted to show a glimpse of white even teeth.

"I'll help." Matt was stoked by the prospect of teaching her to surf. Wow, you and me on board, babe.

"All very well," Matt's father said, addressing Kristy. "What are you studying at the moment?" He showed off his expensive grey knit socks and brown brogue shoes as if to underline what he said.

"Law," she said. "I'm a year ahead of these guys."

"I'm impressed," Matt's father replied. "Talk some sense into Matt, will you?" Again he fidgeted with his cellphone.

Not to be left out, BJ said, "I'm studying drama." He leaned back against the couch with his hands behind his head.

"No future in that," Matt's father said. "What are your other grades like?"

"I don't need good grades. I've got talent." BJ smirked.

Matt's father couldn't control his laughter. "Look out, Hollywood!"

"Don't discourage him," Matt's mother said. "He can join the theatre or go on TV." She sprang to her feet and walked across the living room to the kitchen. At the bench, she clattered dishes into the dishwasher.

"Yeah," Matt said to his mother's back. He found himself agreeing just to annoy his father.

"Small thinking." His father uncrossed his legs and looked in BJ and Kristy's direction.

" I still think you should consider something with more job security," his mother yelled from the kitchen.

"The way of mediocrity," his father replied. "No wonder Matt's the way he is."

"How am I?" Matt glared at his father. Neither his father nor his mother had any idea who he was. How could they? Even he didn't know. But he knew who he wasn't — the guy his father wanted him to be. He wanted him to be an expert number cruncher and follow him into the family business, selling people out to high-risk investors in the prospect of making huge profits, but often losing their money. For now, he had to get out of there. He looked desperately from his mother to BJ and finally jerked his head towards the door. BJ and Kristy took the hint and followed him out. They headed for the beach.

Matt's father yelled after them, "Make sure you're back for lunch."

Matt heard the shriek of seagulls and couldn't take his eyes off them. They swooped between the sand dunes and the North Beach War Memorial Hall and Community Centre. A defiant gull stood on a little boy's lap and pecked at his salad roll, while he put his hands up to his face to protect himself. As the gull attacked the boy's lip in an effort to get a piece of bread, the young mother screamed and waved her arms. Matt grabbed the bird and tried to pull it from the little boy's lap, but it somehow hung on. He flapped his arms and shouted until the gull panicked and flew away. It took half the bread roll with it. The little boy was bleeding from the lip and the mother sponged him with a handkerchief.

"Yaaagh!" the kid cried at the top of his voice.

"Thank you. That was so kind," the mother said, as she calmed the young boy as best she could. "Who says young people are no good?" She waved her arms to stop any other gulls. Matt thought of the student volunteer army that had shovelled away tonnes of liquefaction after the Christchurch earthquakes. Once the food was gone, the gulls lost interest and went to scavenge in other parts of the beach.

"You're welcome," Matt said, as though he did it every day. The onshore wind played in his curly hair. He turned around and scanned the Bowhill Road intersection. The streetscape had really changed since the quakes. The Ozone hotel had gone. There was a gap where the gaudy blue structure with distinctive arched windows once stood. On the opposite side of the road the cute little turreted building overlooking the dunes and beach was also history. It had enjoyed many incarnations from local dairy to a trendy little bar. All gone now.

Matt sauntered over to the beach and held his hand up to shade his eyes. BJ and Kristy followed silently by his side.

He was now very familiar with this area; his father had first brought him here as a toddler. This was the southern section of an eighteen-kilometre stretch of sand that began south of the Waimakariri River. Pegasus Bay fronted the east coast beaches and Christchurch city and arched north.

"Might be better on a fuller tide," BJ said.

Kristy shrugged. "It's OK for me, though."

Matt did not reply. He looked south to New Brighton and the pier, the heart of it all. Originally a coastal village separated from other suburbs by swampy areas and the Avon River, it had suffered badly from the quakes.

The surf had been one constant in an otherwise shaky world. "Yeah, it might get better if the wind changes," he said, and switched his gaze to bathers who had spread themselves on towels on the loose sand around them. A dozen or so surfers were mucking around out the back, either riding or bobbing around like black beans.

BJ stripped his shirt off in the hot sun, exposing rolls of belly flesh.

"Put it back on," Kristy laughed."Whatever." BJ complied.

Matt just blurted it out. "What am I going to do about the old man?"

"I guess that's between you guys," Kristy said. "You have to be you."

"That's right," BJ said, and caught the steely glint in Matt's eyes. "Let him know you're not into his shit."

"Yeah, it's just not me." Matt's focus returned to the waves.

"What would you like to do?" BJ said. Ben Burrows ran past with his board under one arm. BJ high-fived him with his free arm without saying a word.

"I thought you would know by now! A board shaper," Matt said.

BJ's face went red with embarrassment.

"Well, it's simple." Kristy brushed her hair off her

face. "All you have to do is show him you have a firm goal and hopes of a career."

"You don't know my old man. He wants me to carry on his business. He's a total fanatic."

"Tell him your dream," BJ said. "Who knows ...?"

Well, maybe ... but that would all have to wait for now; he was due home for lunch and he didn't want to upset the old man any more today. Besides, his mum would have his lunch ready. She always went to a lot of trouble with cooking.

"I'll catch you two later. Gotta go." He waved over his shoulder as he walked away towards Bowhill Road and his house.

But when Matt arrived home there was no smell of roast chicken, his mother's specialty. She was in the kitchen preparing vegetables, and there was the damp hint of tears in her eyes and on her cheeks. He knew better than to ask her what was wrong; she would no doubt reply she had been peeling onions. So maybe they were going to have lunch later. The old man was slumped on the couch playing on his latest smartphone, checking his emails, Matt guessed.

"Here!" Matt yelled into the kitchen.

"Lunch has been postponed," his father said from the couch, as if it was some sort of sporting event. "I don't think I will be joining you."

Matt frowned. "Why, wassup?"

It must be important, he decided. His father stood up and pointed towards Matt's room.

Matt followed him in, sat on the bed and picked up his guitar; he played a chord sequence. His father closed the door. It shut with a solid clunk like the door of a classic car. Matt placed the guitar beside him and looked at his father, who was sitting opposite in his La-Z-Boy chair that was a bit ratty around the edges. It gave his father a scruffy appearance, which was not in sync with his sports jacket and the trouser crease that you could slice a tomato on.

"There's no easy way to say this." His father averted his gaze and pulled at his trouser leg.

"Say what?" What was so important all of a sudden?

"I'm leaving your mother for another woman."

"Bullshit." Matt stared at him with vacant eyes.

"I'm afraid not, Matthew. It's for real." His father looked at the floor.

An image arose in Matt's mind of all the holidays spent under a wide-open sky with the sun sparkling on the waters like diamonds in the deep green of the sounds — just the three of them. That would never be again. The surfing trips to Bali. The endless days where the sun warmed him while he bathed in tepid waters. That's where the old man introduced him to surfing when he was eight years old. The fishing trips, all over now.

But then his father brought him back to reality. "It could be worse."

"What do you mean?"

"You could come and live with me and Trish." "No way." Matt's heart seemed to miss a beat and his throat gagged. That would never happen. There was no bloody way he would ever go for that.

"Anyway, the house will have to be sold." His father's mouth tightened.

"What about us?"

"You'd be looked after."

"Not this guy. You walk out on me and Mum ... I'm walking out on you." The red flush began at his neck and rose ever higher to his hairline. His chest heaved and his breath came in short bursts. He had a filthy taste in his mouth, and he couldn't hold the words back. "Why do this to us?" He shook, and the words came out in a stifled scream. He didn't recognise his own voice. To his mind, he sounded like an hysterical female. He tossed his guitar on the floor and it gave a dull thud and loud twang.

"Easy," said his father, running a nonchalant hand over his cropped salt and pepper hair.

"Easy? It's easy for you ... you and your floozy." Matt's nostrils flared. Who the heck was she, anyway? Couldn't be his secretary — she was an old tart. He wasn't that desperate. Might be one of his old business buddies, or squash partners. Yeah, that was probably it. They were mostly a youngish upwardly mobile crowd, real pretenders like him.

"It will get better in time." His father's lips twitched at the corners.

Matt sprang from the bed like a scalded cat and formed a fist with his right hand. His whole body tensed. He tapped his instincts, held his fist in his father's face and peered into his impassive grey eyes. "If you weren't my father I'd … I'd beat up on you real bad. From now on I'll make my own way in life."

Yeah, that was it! Make his own way … sounded good, sounded tough, but how the hell was he going to do it? One thing was for sure: he was going to stick by his mother. It was going to be bad for her.

TWO

THE SUN shone on Matt's pillow and his head. He soaked in the rays and rolled over on his back. When he finally opened his eyes, they were sticky with sleep. His cellphone said 9:03 a.m., Saturday. He was glad he had a device for keeping track of the time because of late he didn't know what day it was — let alone the time. The door opened and his mother appeared in her plain blue shift and floral apron, a breakfast tray in her hands. He inhaled the coffee fumes. They were good.

"It's a lovely morning," she said. "I thought you might like a coffee and a piece of toast." She walked over to his bed.

"Thanks." He really had the munchies.

She set the tray down on the bedside table. "I meant to tell you earlier but your father has got a bite on the house."

"Great," he said, not meaning it, "that was quick."

"Things aren't good." There was a hint of water in her eyes. Her mouth twitched, showing a flicker of small white teeth.

"And here's me thinking everything is a box of birds." He picked up the coffee and slurped it.

"I'm going to have to get a job." She sat on the end of the bed.

"Over my dead body."

Matt got a text from BJ to meet him up the beach in ten minutes. The surf was outrageous.

He eased himself out of the conversation as best he could. "Can we talk later? The surf won't wait."

"If you must," she said. "Be careful."

He watched her pick up the tray and make her way back to the kitchen. He chewed on the sweet, gritty toast. His mum was only forty-seven but she had the air of an old woman. This break-up had been tough on her but she was a good mum. He should get a job! She needed help now more than ever. She hadn't worked since her college days.

But, for now, he would head to the beach.

BJ and Kristy were waiting on the beach side of the wooden partition wall at North Beach. The tide had just turned, and was on its way in. The surf was crap. That bloody BJ knew how to get him out of bed in a hurry. It might get better on a fuller tide. There was that chill onshore whipping off the tops of the waves turning them to chop and sending the fine spray on the wind. It would blow into their faces out there.

BJ smiled at Matt.

"You bastard." Matt grabbed him by the scruff of his orange T-shirt.

"Take it easy." BJ shook himself loose. "Lady present."

Kristy stood by BJ with a book tucked under her right arm. She was more beautiful than ever in white jeans and lavender tank top. The book was as thick as a blockbuster novel.

She took the book out, and opened it.

Matt raised an eyebrow. It was her book of poetry. "You gonna read ... between the waves," he stammered and blushed.

"No." She picked up a handful of sand with her free hand, and handed the book to Matt with the other.

He flipped through the pages. "*Auguries of Innocence* ... sounds like heavy stuff." He handed it back to her.

"Yeah, it's by William Blake. It's pretty cool — listen!
To see a World in a Grain of Sand
And a Heaven in a Wild Flower
Hold Infinity in the palm of your hand
And Eternity in an hour".

She let the sand slip through her other hand as if it were an egg timer.

"You outta your tiny mind?" he said.

"Maybe." Kristy gave him a wry smile. She put the book in her bag. "Let's surf."

"OK, you might catch a little wave inshore but it's flat out back."

He'd concentrate on showing Kristy the subtleties of riding the inshore break, that's if BJ was OK with him muscling in. It shouldn't be too bone-crushing today, as the surf was only about waist high and messy.

But first he needed to give her a few of the basics.

Gulls squawked overhead and a steady flow of bathers, all different in age and body size, meandered past. He breathed in noxious exhaust fumes from the hoons' cars that squealed around the intersection facing the North Beach War Memorial Hall.

They untied the boards from the Hilux and took them over to the beach. Matt pulled his towel around himself and shimmied into his wetsuit behind the granite wall that separated them from a green area, a curvaceous female nude sculpture and the car park. He shuddered with cold even though it was a summer's day, and goose bumps formed on his arms.

He watched BJ and Kristy as they wriggled into their wetties, towel round their waists to avoid exposing themselves to the world. Kristy wore an old wetsuit of his that he had when he was a kid before any major growth spurts. It fitted OK, just a bit loose in the shoulders. And BJ had given her his old board that had a few dings on the rails from being tossed around on the roof rack over the years; there was a major one on the nose as well, where BJ had pranged into another surfer one time. It was ideal for a newbie — long and wide. In his mind's eye he was already seeing Kristy on her board paddling in a frenzied way whenever a decent-sized curl formed. He would show her how it was done.

"OK, Kristy, lie face down on your board."

"What? On the sand?"

"Yup. I want you to go from lying down to standing up in one action."She stood up. "Like this."

"Good. Bend your knees slightly."

She did.

"Great. Now I want you to imagine your board is a little boat with an outboard motor."

"Are you crazy?" BJ said.

"The power comes from behind and so does the steering. You apply pressure with your back foot and lean slightly into where you want to go. You accelerate with your front foot."

"Easy, Avery, she can't even stand up yet."

"Yeah … I reckon that's enough for starters."

But his dreams were to be short-lived. They had to give up in disgust after only the first few attempts, because the waves were just too chopped up to ride. But Kristy did manage to stand up on one. They had wasted their time going out. It was really just for paddling practice.

At the water's edge BJ ran into Jake Edwards from the school basketball team. Edwards leered at him. "Hello, fat man," he said and pushed BJ in the chest. BJ dropped his board. He fell to the wet sand, shivering all over, and went pale in the face.

Matt let his board fall in the shallows, ran up to Edwards and grabbed him by his muscle shirt. He looked him in the eye and said, "How'd you like to try that on me?"

He knew he could take Edwards any time he wanted. And he could tell by the cowed look in Edwards' eye he knew that too. It was second nature to him to defend himself and others. He had trained for it in the local dojo for the last ten years. He had had a black belt for the last two, but didn't feel the need to go any higher; he had the skills to take on most bullies. They didn't take much. They were all piss and wind.

"Stay out of it," Edwards said. "This is nothing to do with you, tough guy."

"Anyone who picks on my friends has a fight with me." Matt spoke through his teeth with a hiss.

Kristy brought Matt's board out of the shallows, holding a board under each arm.

On Kristy's approach Edwards backed away and said, "You can't protect him all the time." He scarpered over to the beach car park and got into his Subaru wagon.

"You should never resort to violence," Kristy said. Her face glowed and her green eyes sparkled.

"You don't sound like you mean it." Matt kicked at the sand.

"I would have been toast," BJ said.

"Speaking of toast," Matt said, "I'm getting hungry." They walked back to pick up their clothes and take them up the sand dunes. They sat down on the dunes with a view of the dirty churned-up sea.

"The thing is," Matt looked into the distance, "I need a job."

"The old man might need a car groomer." BJ leaned back into the sand dune.

"Nah." Matt yawned with hands above his head.

"They are looking for people in Produce at my work," Kristy said.

"Can you get me an application?" The last thing he wanted to do was stack shelves in a supermarket, but if it meant working with Kristy ... well, that was different.

"Sure." Kristy dug her poetry book out of her bag.

"OK, I'll shoot home and check out my CV."

"Cool. Catcha later," BJ and Kristy said at the same time.

The smell of something cooking filled the house when Matt barged through the front door. Whatever it was it had his taste buds doing somersaults.

"Just in time." His mother stood at the stove and stirred the pot of baked beans. It was simple grub but he loved it. Baked beans and eggs on toast always went down a treat after a surf, even if it was a non-event. He sat down at the table in the kitchen and his mother placed the meal in front of him. Though she sat at the head of the table, she was not eating.

He worried about her, but it did not affect his appetite. His stomach had that rumbling empty feel and he wolfed the eggs and beans down. It filled the gnawing gap. His mother seemed stauncher now, and he was sure she would eventually come to terms with her situation.

She would have to.

He put his knife and fork down and looked at his mother, who pushed her hair back from her face and caught his eye. "Things are worse than I thought." She played with her place mat that had a lake scene on it in an effort to avoid facing facts. "Your father always handled the finances. It seems the mortgage was bigger than I realised. I come out with very little and we have to get another house. We might even have to rent."

"We'll do what we have to do," Matt said. "I'll help." He stood up and put his arm around her shoulder. "Have you seen my CV?" Such as it was — it only had two jobs on it: one delivering the local newspaper, and one after-school job at Jackson's Hardware where the staff amused themselves by having him on. They sent him out for sky hooks and long weights and thought it was a hell of a joke. His father thought it would be character building. Showed what he knows.

"I think it's in the hall desk drawer." She put her hand on his shoulder and he shrugged it off.

He rummaged in the desk drawer. It wasn't hard to find; it was in one of those big brown manila envelopes. He took it out and could see there was a year since his last job. He was going to do it hard.

He wanted to leave his options open, and only take Kristy's supermarket job as a last resort; they only paid minimum wage. He really wanted to become a board shaper and eventually go into his own business.

Average Economics results would be OK for that. Once his talents were recognised he could see himself being a big success. "I found it," he yelled, and took it into the living room where his mother was.

She sat on the couch. "I'm glad you found it." She put on the glasses that hung on a chain around her neck. "Can I have a look?"

He handed her the CV. "It's pretty basic." He thought of his father's contempt for anything average. Just how average might he end up, and would his efforts be enough to save his mother and himself from what seemed like certain ruin?

THREE

MATT GLANCED at the digital clock on his bedside table. It was 8.30 Monday morning — as good a time as any to look for work. He had an appointment downtown with Wexford & Todd, building contractors. They paid good money for builder's labourers because the work could be dangerous, and they were really in demand. He lay there on his stomach with his body wracked from heavy surfing and all the cares of the world that never used to affect him. His mouth was dry and tasted foul; he could use a sugary drink. He rolled over on his back and contemplated getting out of bed. The events of the last week or so ran like a movie in his head. He hated to see his mother in the state she was in. Not only had she been deserted and left in a financial bind, but he was all she had for support; his father had done his best to alienate any friends she had, and her close family all lived out of town.

He snatched his cellphone from the bedside table. He thought he heard it go off when he was halfway between sleep and semi-consciousness. He was right. It was a message from BJ to say he would meet him up the beach later. Matt had news for him. He could forget about surfing for the day and be his taxi around Christchurch. It was never a straightforward drive into town: the roads were corrugated, slumped and full of potholes. There was no such thing as a direct route. You had to go out of your way to get a through road to where you were going. The traditional direct routes and one-way systems were often kaput and gated off with wire mesh. Orange road cones were everywhere. The city area still looked like the result of a World War Two blitzkrieg, and this was years after the 2011 earthquake.

He would set his sights high. Maybe he could start out making coffee till he learnt the intricacies of big-time contracting. Then he could do what he really loved — shaping boards with Jack Dawson, who used to surf with his old man in their heyday. Christchurch was a small world when it came down to it; his old man knew everybody. It was sort of the old school tie thing with a twist.

Matt sent BJ a text to pick him up in half an hour, and his mother floated into the room with a coffee that smelled rich and beany. She handed it to him.

"It seems the sale of the house has gone through. We've got a month to get out."

Matt took a deep breath. "The prick."

"Don't say that about your father." She frowned and blinked her hazel eyes.

"I don't think of him that way any more." Matt drained the last of his coffee and placed the cup on the bedside table. He wrenched the covers back and slid out of bed wearing a black T-shirt and pyjama pants with surfboard motifs on them.

He showered and soaked in the hot spray that soothed his aching shoulders. He dried off and slipped into his best pants, shirt and leather jacket. He had a mouthful of minty toothpaste when he heard the toot-toot that he recognised as BJ's horn.

It was a slow trip downtown past the road works, potholes, slumps and detours. The receptionist at Wexford & Todd, a pretty brunette with bright-red lipstick, took Matt's details. Behind her was a picture on the wall of hard hats lunching on a steel girder high in the sky oblivious to any danger. They were completely relaxed and dangled their limbs in midair.

She smelt of violets. "Mr Wexford is expecting you. Please take a seat, and I will let him know you are here," she said.

Matt sat down. The waiting room had floor-to-ceiling panoramic views overlooking Oxford Terrace. His larger outlook was obscured by two glass towers. Somewhere beyond them lay the Botanic Gardens and just this side of them the Arts Centre, the original Canterbury University site. Almost the whole place had been red-stickered after the second quake, which meant demolition and unsuitability for construction.

But there had been a change of plans. These heritage Gothic Revival buildings were now being restored and strengthened. By 2019 they should again be a centre for the arts, culture and creativity and lead the way in the wider Christchurch rebuild.

In the foreground was the Avon River and a mish-mash of empty plots among survivors that looked a bit like gapped teeth in a once-aristocratic mouth. It was sad to see so many heritage buildings gone. Just in front of him, over the river the old Venetian Gothic library was no more. His mother used to point out a lot of these types of buildings.

Wexford's door opened and out popped a suave grey head. "Sorry to keep you, Matt. I've been waylaid by an important client. Won't be a minute." He withdrew his head inside like a turtle into its shell.

"You can go in now, Mr Avery," the receptionist said.

Wexford sat in the power position behind a substantial oak and leather desk and waved at Matt to take a seat. Matt ran a cursory eye over Wexford while Wexford eyed him in turn. He looked like an aged film star in an Armani suit or some other up-market label. Matt wasn't an expert on designer clothes. And from where he sat he got a faint whiff of hair gel, or was it aftershave?

"So …" He had Matt's CV in his hand; he had obviously been reading it before he came in. "Avery — I know that name well. Alec, I presume, is your father?"

"Yes, that's right," Matt said and squirmed inside. He shifted in his seat.

Wexford eyeballed Matt. "I would have thought Avery and Associates would have been your first port of call."

"It's a long story, but I was hoping I would be taken on my own merits." He looked out the window.

"Or lack of them," Wexford said. A wry smile played on his thin lips.

"Yes, well, I have to start somewhere."

"Agreed," Wexford said. "But it's that old chestnut. Employers are looking for workers with experience and applicants are looking to get experience. Your grades are not spectacular, but we go a lot on common sense around here. You seem a personable young man, but I make no promises."

Matt smiled. "Thank you."

"I will get back to you." He slipped out of his chair with the litheness of a young man. "Let me walk you out." He placed a fatherly hand on Matt's shoulder. Matt flinched. "You realise, should you be successful, we will be grooming you for a career in the construction industry. Who knows, maybe you will be sitting behind my desk one day."

Matt cringed inside. He was in it for the short term.

He couldn't believe it! As Wexford walked him into the reception area, his father and, he presumed, the delectable Trish were standing there. His father wore a dark suit and had a briefcase in his hand. Trish was dressed in a tight black leather skirt and red blouse, which showed off plenty of flesh and gold bling. He had to admit she was hot for an older woman. They chattered and laughed. When Matt's father saw him, he said, "The offer is still open."

"You'd be very welcome," Trish said. She smiled wide.

"Not interested." He held his head high and strode past them, getting a blast of Trish's sexy perfume on the way out. Wexford didn't mention anything in the interview about them, but then, he supposed he wouldn't.

BJ straddled a footpath bench as he ogled the passing female population. Matt arrived. The Hilux with surfboards up top was in a metered park in front of them. They could still catch a surf. Matt just had to convince BJ of that after rejecting him earlier. He sat in silence next to BJ, thinking about the truck his father would have bought him if he'd scored an A in Economics instead of a C+. He had the indignity of having a licence but being reliant on his mate for transport. His mother was reluctant to let him drive her new breed VW beetle. It was her last link with some sort of status.

Matt and BJ pulled into the car park at North Beach. They took their boards and wetsuits and wandered over to the dunes and were surprised to see Kristy sunbathing in the gap between the memorial hall and the dunes. Her board lay askew at her feet and the poetry book was in her hand. She seemed totally oblivious to everything around her, even the raucous gulls overhead. She was supposed to be at work. They sauntered over to her and stood between her and the sun, which made her look up at them.

"No work today?" she asked.

Matt sat down beside her. "Something like that."

She shut her book and placed it in her bag. "I'm doing nights stacking shelves; gives me time to surf."

"That's cool," BJ said. He sat on the other side of her.

She foraged in her string beach bag and pulled out a job application form. She turned to Matt.

"I got you this."

"Thanks." He took it. "But I don't think I'll need it now I got a job coming up at Wexford & Todd."

Kristy raised her eyebrows. "The contractors?" Her lips curled up at the corners and her green eyes twinkled. "After the danger money?"

"Yeah. I need it bad." He watched two surfers catch the same wave and ride it to shore.

Gulls were rising and falling on the thermals out the back. As if she were speaking to the gulls, she said: "… *With my cross-bow I shot the Albatross.*"

"What are you talking about?" Matt said.

Kristy seemed to ignore BJ and turned her attention to Matt. "Those gulls just reminded me of something: the irrational shooting of the albatross by the Ancient Mariner. In the poem, Coleridge says that the Mariner is well aware he is doing something stupid but does it anyway. He knows it's going to turn out bad, and he'll have to pay for it."

Matt's eyes glazed over.

Kristy took a deep breath. "Don't shoot down the prospects of getting a more suitable job to go after a fast buck. Don't be stupid. Think of the consequences, and don't do it. You could always bury your pride and go work for your father … just as a means to an end. You don't have to sacrifice your values." She bit her lip. "I'll tell you what: you keep on teaching me the finer points of surfing and I'll lend you my poetry book." Kristy smiled and her eyes lit up.

"It sounds like you're getting the better end of the deal," Matt said. "And anyway, it's not a question of pride. No bloody way will I ever work for my old man, after the way he treated me and Mum. I'm just worried about the short-term cash flow."

"Sorry, I just thought it might be a temporary fix, that's all." She shrugged her shoulders.

"Hey, I thought teaching Kristy to surf was my job," BJ said.

"You can both help me," she said.

"OK, deal," Matt said. He watched the beach scene unfold in front of him and breathed in the salty air. His only experience of poetry was being forced to listen to his parents spout Shelley on their trailer sailer in the sounds. All he could remember was his father quoting what he thought was something to do with anarchy and Shelley. That was in their student days. And he remembered his father reciting:

"… *Tis to work and have such pay*
As just keeps life from day to day"

Something like that … but in his later years he had never heard him mention poetry. If he did, it was to put it down — the way he dealt with most of the arts, with the exception of the visual arts where there could be quite a bit of money to be made.

Kristy gave Matt the book of poetry, and he wrapped it in his towel. He stood up and checked out the surf, a nice little wave peeling left and right. It would be good for Kristy. Jake Edwards walked past and gave BJ the finger. Kristy yelled back to him, "Bully!"

Kobe, a friend from school, drove past on Marine Parade in his fibreglass beach buggy, his ginger hair all over the place as though he had just got out of bed. It was three o'clock in the afternoon. He parked his car and a few minutes later came over to Matt, blatantly smoking a joint. "Want a toke?"

"Sure, why not?" Matt said.

Matt and BJ passed the joint back and forth. Kobe pulled two cigar-shaped articles from his jacket pocket wrapped in tinfoil. "Want to buy some? Twenty bucks a throw."

"Sure," Matt said. "It might help me to chill out."

"Don't be stupid," Kristy said. "That stuff kills motivation."

"Must be good then."

A police car turned at the Memorial Hall intersection, but, lucky for them, they were in hot pursuit, their blue and red light flashing but no siren. They must have wanted to surprise someone, Matt thought. His head was in a good space now the weed had taken the sharp edge off. But then he saw his mother's Beetle pull up at the intersection and he remembered. The surf would have to wait. He had promised her he would check out some rental properties with her, but it was early days yet. They still had plenty of time before they had to get out. He was glad she didn't see him smoking the weed. She had enough on her plate.

Financial pressures were beginning to bite. He needed an income stream, fast! He hated to see his mother going back to work. She had found a job cooking at Christchurch Public Hospital, and he didn't like her having to do that when she was a trained professional. It's just that the world had moved on since her days as a librarian. She would need to retrain to get a decent job, which would cost money rather than generate it. He would make sure she didn't have to do it for long.

FOUR

THE SUN burned hot on Matt's shoulders as he sat with BJ and Kristy in the Brighton Mall on the bench seats under the windblown phoenix palms. The smell of sausages and onions on the wind stirred his appetite. People dawdled past in all their rainbow colours and various stages of undress. They looked about as scruffy and off balance as the buildings that survived the quakes. Pathetic little grommets weaved in and out of them on their skateboards. He should tell them to pack it in before they ran someone over. They had his attention now. What else was there to do when the surf was crap?

He and his mum still had to find a house to rent. So far the houses they had looked at were not much better than dog kennels. A lot still needed earthquake commission work, and they wanted a bucket of gold for them. The quakes had pushed the rent for available houses sky high.

Saturday afternoons in Brighton were like this: all those aimless nine-to-fivers soaking up their little bit of weekend freedom.

Kristy was dressed in a yellow tank top and short denim skirt. Matt thought she looked hot but he would never tell her. She might think he was some sort of goof. BJ slouched in his baggy shorts and hoodie; you could tell he used to be a skater boy before he took to the surf. A stray shaggy-haired dog came up and sniffed around them. Matt looked at Kristy and remembered a line from Blake's Auguries of Innocence, one of the poems from her poetry book, and part of the poem she had quoted to him earlier. He thought it might impress.

"A dog starv'd at his Master's Gate
Predicts the ruin of the State."

Kristy's eyes sparkled green and her lips curled up at the ends. "You've been reading the book!" The dog rested his nose on her knees. She scragged his ears. The dog gave a little sniff and whined.

"I might have," Matt said. He patted the mangy collie on the head. "I wish I could take you home, boy." The dog jumped up, putting a paw on each shoulder, and tried to lick him. He pushed him down, but the dog was persistent.

"He's hungry," BJ said. "Let's get him a couple of sausages. They'll have a sausage sizzle around here. You can smell it."

"Good idea," Matt said. "You go and get them."

"Cool," BJ said.

Matt watched BJ disappear into the crowd as a middle-aged couple approached. He recognised them as Kristy's parents. They came on over. Kristy's father was a white-haired man about his late forties. Her mother had a French bob and had big boobs but looked about ten years younger. He had only ever seen them from a distance when he and BJ had dropped Kristy at her house. Kristy introduced them as Bob and Mary, but Matt stuck to calling them Mr and Mrs Jamieson.

The collie sniffed around the oldies, and Matt pulled him back. His face went red with embarrassment when the dog poked his nose in Kristy's mother's crotch. Kristy stifled a giggle and Mr Jamieson pretended not to see. The dog settled after a while and the parents sat down either side of Kristy but turned their attention to Matt.

"So, uni starts soon," Mr Jamieson said. He focused on Matt and he ran a bony hand through his shock of white hair.

"That's next year," said Matt. "But I won't be going."

"Not going? I wonder what your parents think of that." Mr Jamieson's brow wrinkled. There was a low rumble like a motorcycle starting and then they saw and heard the shop fronts rattle. It lasted only a few seconds but felt much longer to Matt.

"Did you feel that?" said Mr Jamieson. "That was about a 3.5. We were lucky in our part of Fendalton, not much damage."

BJ arrived back with sausages. "We weren't so lucky. We lost the south wall of our house."

"Our place has been repaired." Matt looked for support from Kristy and Mary but there was only silence.

He tried to ignore talk of the quake. "My dad left home." He looked down at the pavement.

"I don't even notice those shakes now," said BJ.

"I do," said Kristy.

"They are very unsettling … " Mrs Jamieson said. .

Bob Jamieson ignored her. "I'm sorry to hear about your father. But you mustn't give up on a tertiary education."

"You don't need one to make surfboards," Matt said.

"I see," Mr Jamieson said. "Come on, Mary, we must leave these young people to their devices. I have some clients' files to go over." He turned to Kristy. "I think you should come too. Did you forget your cousin was coming over to talk courses for this year?"

"But the guys are taking me surfing later. Blast, I forgot about Sharon." She folded her arms.

"Another day, perhaps." Mr Jamieson turned to Matt. "Nice to meet you," he said.

BJ held out two sausages. The collie jumped up and devoured them in one action.

"A bit of respite from your studies, eh, BJ?" Mr Jamieson said.

"For sure," BJ replied.

The Jamiesons sauntered away with Kristy, joining the crowd, the collie trotting after them.

"Let's go and see what's happening at the pier," Matt said.

Matt watched the passing tide of people going the other way, as he and BJ joined the trickle of people going to the beach. The surf must still be crap, he thought. The day was hot and his throat was dry. Here and there little whirlwinds picked up the sand, lolly papers and fast-food wrappers and deposited them all along the pavement.

The smells from the fast food were everywhere and Matt smelt onions in particular. Crowds thronged onto the pier that was dotted with fishermen with their rods raised skywards. The library was closed, but the café was getting its fair share of customers.

Matt and BJ wandered down to the beach. Matt could see there were no surfers out in the waves. The surf was a short chop. There was usually a nice little wave just left of the pier, but it was shit today. The waves did not look like they would improve any time soon. They should check out what was happening over at the cenotaph. It was another one of those places they chilled when the surf was bad.

Matt sighted a huddle of guys around the monument. It had been tagged over the plaque dedicated to 'our glorious dead'. It seemed to Matt a real kick in the teeth to those poor old soldiers that had fought in terrible wars for the country's freedom.

But then his cynical side kicked in. He had heard it said by dissenters that the only reason they have war monuments is so they can do it all again. The other guys were smoking and drinking and yahooing. They got a surprise when he and BJ approached.

"Wassup, guys?" Burrows said. "What say we go and get more comfortable on the steps?" The steps formed a semicircle that faced the basketball court and backed onto the cenotaph.

'I thought we might drop in and see what's going down."

"Not much," Kobe said, walking towards the steps. "Want a smoke?" He waved a piece of tinfoil. "I'll put it on your tab."

"Cool," Matt and BJ said at the same time.

Matt unfurled the foil and took a cigarette paper from Kobe. He rolled a nice tight joint, and lit it from the end of the one Ben Burrows smoked. He took in a deep toke and passed it to BJ. Every cell of his body seemed to soak it up as if he were starving for a special medicine that made his deepest concerns melt into the recesses of his mind. He toked again and it warmed him inside and turned every thought hilarious.

He could hear himself laughing as if he were eavesdropping on his own thoughts. It was heads. Good strong stuff. He didn't care about his old man, his mother, or anything. He was just cruising, freewheeling for a while. They all sat on the steps.

"Where's the girl today?" Ben Burrows slugged a mouthful of lager from the bottle in his hand.

Matt took a deep puff of smoke and blew it out. "With her olds."Burrows smirked. "She's quite a little hottie. I wouldn't mind —"

Matt cut him short. "We are just mates."

"Good." Burrows twisted the top of a new bottle of beer. "It's open season then."

"I guess so." Matt's mouth turned down and his eyes narrowed. He inhaled the last of the joint and threw it down. His mouth tasted like the night after a raging party. He got up from the steps. "C'mon, BJ, let's check out the surf shop in the mall."

"Sure," BJ said, facing the huddle. "Catch you guys later."

"Not if I see you first," Burrows yelled back at them with a playful note in his voice.

Matt cast an eye over the latest surfboards and wetsuits in the window of Dawson's Custom Boards. He didn't much like going into the store because the shop assistants usually pounced on him and talked down to him like he was an absolute grommet. Brighton had lost about eighteen commercial buildings in the quakes. This was a new building that had risen from the ashes like a phoenix. He liked to browse through the latest board shorts and tees. He was drawn to labels like Rip Curl, O'Neill, Billabong; he had bought a nice dark-green plaid-patterned O'Neill jacket from them. It had been a good hard-wearing one that kept him warm after many a surf.

Jack Dawson, the owner of the store, had been one of his father's surfing mates but Matt had never met him.

He had heard his father talk about him being a bit of a dreamer and not much of a businessman but a terrific surfer and board shaper. But Jack seemed to be doing all right for himself now.

Matt and BJ checked out some steamers when a thin man with straggly grey hair approached them. "Can I help you boys?"

"We're just looking." Matt had a wetsuit in his hand. He realised it was Jack Dawson himself. Matt had heard the shop assistants refer to him as Jack on other visits.

Jack picked up another suit and unzipped the back. "These are a good mid-range suit."

"I'd love one, but I'm a bit short of funds at the moment." Matt laughed and hung the suit back on the rack.

"Haven't I seen you boys around at North Beach?" He zipped the wetsuit up and laid it on a display unit.

"Yup," BJ said. "That's our main haunt."

Jack turned to Matt. "You have a familiar look about you; you're not Alec Avery's boy, are you?"

"Yeah. Sorry to say."

"We used to surf together when we were kids," Jack said.

Matt took in a deep breath and exhaled with a whoosh. He decided now was the time to put it to Jack while he had his full attention. "I've always dreamed of being a board shaper. Have you got any vacancies?"

Jack raised his eyebrows. "I wish I did, but I just took

on an apprentice. And I've had a lot of extra expenditure since the quakes."

"Will you keep me in mind?" Matt looked at the ground.

"I'll do better than that." Jack cleared his throat. "I can give you a bit of experience cleaning the shaping bays and glassing rooms. I'll give you a blank to practise on in payment. Then maybe we can review the job situation. See how you work out. By the way, if you don't already know, I'm Jack, Jack Dawson, and before you decide to rib me … yes, I'm the namesake of the Leonardo DiCaprio character in *Titanic*."

"That's cool." Matt's lips formed a broad smile. But he was well aware it didn't solve his cash-flow problem. It would only be voluntary work for now. It was a crazy coincidence about his name.

FIVE

MATT TOOK the letter out of the box and the Wexford & Todd logo told him it was the reply from his recent job interview. His fingers trembled as he tore it open. It should be good news. He reckoned he had impressed. When he opened and unfolded it, his mouth dropped. It was the same old computer-generated thing: 'Thank you for your interest in the position at Wexford & Todd Construction. Unfortunately, your application has been unsuccessful. We wish you every success in the future.' So it was back to square one. He couldn't help it; one of those vicious thoughts came to mind. I bet they hired someone from out of town. But then reality took over. It looked like he would be applying for the supermarket job after all.

His mother was in the kitchen making a coffee when he came back in. She looked over at him. "Not good news?" She walked across to the couch and sat down. She patted the couch to invite him to sit beside her.

"No … it's a rejection from Wexford & Todd." He sat down beside her.

"Never mind. We could use the money. But I would have worried about you all the time."

"I'm going to take my CV and application into that new supermarket over near the estuary this afternoon."

"That's a waste of your education and talents, dear."

"We don't have a choice." He stood up and looked out the window at the beach traffic. His lean frame was silhouetted in the picture window.

She spoke to his back. "We have to find a rental too. We're out in a week". She took a deep breath. He turned around and thought she looked frumpy in the pink leisure suit, so much older than her forty-seven years.

"The agent wants to show me that old shack down Marine Parade."

"I guess it would be a roof over our heads, and it's handy to everything."

"It's all we can afford."

Matt knew she was out of her comfort zone. Since they had been a family, his mother had never had to take the full brunt of the economic facts of life. His father had always allowed her to be wrapped in cotton wool and let her keep up appearances in ways she was used to. He would leave the appointment with the agent to his mother.

He had been in that house before. Jamie Whittle from school used to live there. It was a real surfer's shack with views of the sea through the gaps in the dunes. It even had its own outdoor sink and bench for gutting fish and a corrugated iron outside shower for getting the sand off after a surf. It had a proper bathroom inside as well and an old tumble-down garage that was good for hanging out in and storing his gear. He didn't need to be persuaded, but it would be a big come-down for his mum.

He spun around to look at his mother. "I'm going to drop my CV in at the supermarket."

"All right, dear. I suppose I should wish you luck."

Matt was reduced to his old push-bike; BJ was busy. The supermarket was abuzz with midday shoppers when Matt burst through the self-opening doors. He watched as mothers and toddlers, pensioners, couples, the morbidly obese and the anorexic picked from the shelves and cruised the aisles. They were in a world of their own, stocking the pantry for another week.

He marched up to the desk where they sold Lotto tickets and got the attention of a young brunette with her hair tied back.

"Who will I give my job application to?" he said.

"You want Rick." She pointed at a guy in his mid-thirties with slicked-back black hair. He was over by the eggs with a slim red-headed girl.

"Thank you." He turned on his heel and strode over to Rick with butterflies in his stomach.

The red-headed girl was just walking away with a carton of eggs in her hand when Matt approached. "Excuse me."

"What is it?" Rick snapped.

"I'd like to apply for the shelf-stacking job." The

butterflies in his stomach had turned into dragonflies. He held out the documents and Rick took them.

"It's your lucky day. I've just had two staff walk out on me." He cast an eye over Matt's jeans and black T-shirt. "We will expect you to wear a uniform."

"That's fine." Matt smiled. "You mean I've got the job?"

"If your referees turn out OK, you can start tomorrow afternoon at four p.m. I'll ring you."

Matt took in a big breath. The dragonflies had stopped buzzing. It was too easy. Things might be looking up. He would go to see Kristy in Produce and tell her the news.

Kristy was bent over her flatbed trolley unloading oranges into the display bin when Matt disturbed her. "I think I got the job."

She finished placing the oranges on the second tier of the bin and spun around to face him. "That's good. When do you start?" The air was filled with a sharp citrus smell that tickled his nose.

"Tomorrow, if my CV checks out."

"That's good."

Matt wondered how long she could stick this type of job. "What do you want do in the future?"

"My olds want me to be a lawyer, but I want to teach." She finished topping up the bin and moved along to the mandarins.

"My teachers sucked." He was reminded of Mr Locke, his Science teacher who used to rap the kids over the knuckles with a ruler when he wanted their attention. It was a wonder Locke got away with it for so long, but he did.

"That may be, but I want to make a difference. If you keep focused and have ambition, it's amazing how you can overcome pathetic teachers." She heaved the cartons onto the trolley. Her small frame strained at every lift.

"Yeah, well, good luck is all I can say."

"Don't you have any ambition?"

"For sure. I want to shape surfboards." And in his mind he was off on a glassy wave cutting through it on a thruster he had designed and shaped.

"That's sounds like fun," she said.

He left her to finish her shift and biked home. He stopped at home long enough to drop his bike and get his surfing gear. By now his mother would be working at the hospital. He sent a text to BJ to meet him up the beach and enjoyed the thought that he was still free enough to surf. He might as well chill out while he could.

At North Beach he put his board and wetsuit down by the granite wall. He leaned against it and watched the surf out the back. The Burrows brothers were there and so was Jake Edwards. He figured it was about time he gave BJ another martial arts lesson to take that hotshot Edwards down.

BJ pulled up in his Hilux in the car park and made his way over to where Matt leaned on the wall. Matt turned around and saw him coming. "The surf's piss poor …

and Edwards is out there."

"That dweeb." BJ's jaw dropped.

"Let's go over to Thomsons Park and practise a few kicks and punches," Matt said.

"OK, why not? That douchebag isn't going to scare me any more." BJ threw a punch that looked like slapping someone's face with a wet fish.

"That's the attitude. Let's go." There were three young kids on the swings while a couple looked on. Matt thought they were the parents because there was no one else around. He found a flat area of grass away from them and put BJ through his moves.

"Think of your body with a centre line down the middle, and you are punching at that line. Pull your fist into your chest about nipple height and twist it out forward to that line in a screwing sort of motion. Do the same with both arms." He held the palm of his hands out in front of BJ to act as a punching bag. "Aim for those. I can take it." BJ's limp punches made little impact on his hands, but every now and then BJ would land one that stung. "Now use your feet. See if you can land a front kick on me."

BJ gave an almighty front kick with his right foot. He fell hard on his backside.

Matt laughed. "Edwards doesn't have to beat you up. You're doing a good job of it yourself."

BJ lay on the sandy grass and glared up at him. "I'll show him — and you."

"OK, let's head back to the beach." Matt pulled BJ to his feet.

They met Edwards at the sea wall in his wetsuit with a board under one arm. He was fresh out of the water and stopped in front of BJ. "It beats me why your surfboard doesn't sink. I mean, with all that lard above the waterline." Edwards smirked.

"Lay off," Matt said.

"Yeah, lay off!" BJ pushed Edwards in the chest and he reeled backwards.

Matt took hold of BJ's arm. He didn't know where he got the courage from, unless it was from the latest lesson. Edwards went to land one on BJ but stopped. He must have realised it wasn't a good idea.

"You'll keep, Jolly. Your minder won't always be around."

"Keep on dreaming, dirtbag." Matt looked him straight in his murky eyes.

"Ditto," BJ said.

"I can wait, fatso." He gave them both the finger and walked over to the surf club car park.

Matt watched him go, glad to see the back of him. As far as he was concerned, Edwards was a coward and a bully. Those types usually got their dues sooner or later. That's why he intended to tutor BJ in the finer points of the martial arts. BJ had only had a few lessons, but already his confidence was boosted. He still had a long way to go, but he would harden up OK.

Trouble was, if he got that job at the supermarket he might not be around as much to defend BJ. But this wasn't the only reason he felt uneasy about the job. Rick had already had two workers walk out on him, and he more or less employed him on the spot. Maybe there was a good reason for the staff turnover. He hoped it would turn out all right and he could help his mother out. He had an uneasy feeling about Rick. But for now the surf would wash away his cares. Matt turned to BJ. "Last one in's a flabby dweeb."

SIX

"THANKS, GUYS. Couldn't have done it without you." Matt slapped BJ and Kobe on the back, shook hands formally with the Burrows brothers, and turned to survey the pile of boxes and oddments of furniture that now littered the bare rooms of their new house in Marine Parade. His mother smiled broadly and handed him money to shout them all a burger down at New Brighton before he went to work.

They all bundled into the Hilux and hurtled off in the direction of Brighton. It was cool now they were in the new house and a big relief. It meant freedom from his old man. His father had said he would be there to give them a hand — yeah right, other more important business must have come up. Typical! They decided on Subway, the healthy option, and went to park up the Ramp, a car park area overlooking the pier and Brighton Beach, to eat the rolls. There were two Ramps. This was the northern one. The other one was by the cenotaph on the other side of the pier.

The cool easterly wind Brighton is known for blew onshore and gave Matt goose pimples on his forearms. He knew, from school, Maori had a couple of names for the area. One of those was O-rua-paeroa, which means 'an east wind blowing along the shore'. The second was something about food and yellow-eyed mullet. One out of two didn't seem too bad for a guy who wasn't good with other languages. Matt watched the wind pick up their Subway wrappers and scatter them along the beach. He felt a twinge of guilt. They weren't very good conservationists.

He looked over to the pier. It stretched out about 300 metres, past the waves today. There were several fishermen at the end of the pier waving their rods around. But it didn't have any sideshows or arcade machines like he knew they had in places like Blackpool or Brighton in the UK. That's what they named New Brighton after. It would be cool to have entertainment on this pier.

Seagulls landed on the Hilux. The gulls were used to frequenting this car park for easy pickings. They shrieked and stood on the hood looking in at them as if to coerce them into giving them pieces of their foot-longs. Matt had his window down and the wind flicked back his hair and blew the appetising food smells around the car. He heard the steady rumble of motorcycles close by. The riders came up the Ramp in pairs and parked their bikes behind them. He became wary as the bearded leader, the one they called Snake, and another known as Mullet, approached the car. He watched them in the side mirror.

Snake tapped on the roof of the car. "Good day for it."

Matt didn't answer. Snake turned his attention to Kobe. "I hope you're not dealing your filthy weed on our patch." Snake eyeballed them all. "Otherwise I won't be responsible for the actions of my boys."

"I wouldn't do that," Kobe said.

"Well, make sure you don't. Ya know my motto?" Snake said. "The only good surfer's a dead one, but their ladies are all right."

Snake started to walk back to his bike, then turned around. "We don't take easy to being crossed with drugs."

"Whatever," Matt said.

His eyes followed the bikers, who sauntered back to their bikes, and there was the collective rumble of a dozen motorbikes bursting into life. They reverberated in his solar plexus. There was no way they would put the frighteners on him or hassle his friends.

He looked at his cellphone. It was 3.30 p.m. and he had to be at work at 4. Rick had phoned while they were in the middle of the move and asked him to start that afternoon.

He got BJ to drop him at the supermarket door amidst the comings and goings of eager shoppers.

The iodine smell from the estuary hit him fully in the senses.

Matt watched the Hilux disappear out of the car park, and stood inhaling the toxic fumes from BJ's exhaust. He wished he could have stayed with them but work was like that. It was the great destroyer of fun. In fact, it seemed to him rather like a prison where you got to go home at night. What made it worse, it was Saturday night, his usual night for chilling out. It meant it would be crowded, and he'd have to dodge customers as he filled shelves, and they could get schizoid when you got in their way.

Rick was waiting at the bottom of the stairs ready to give him his night's work.

Matt was soon in the aisles topping up the dog and cat food when his father and Trish came along for their pedigree dog food for Trish's bichon frise that she carried everywhere like some upmarket accessory. This time she had left the dog out in the Jag. They had parked right up to the front of the shop, and Matt could see and hear the dog yapping at passers-by through the plate-glass window.

"Good that you are busy at work on a Saturday night. That's real dedication for you ..." Matt's father leaned over and took two boxes of dog food that Matt had just put on the shelf. "The sort we could use at Avery Associates."

Trish took one of the boxes and looked at the fine print as she squinted through her glasses. "We thought we would try out the new supermarket. You should listen to your father."

"I'm quite happy here." Matt bit his lip. He was overcome by Trish's cloying musk perfume. It packed a real wallop. She must have put heaps on. One smell to cover up another, he reckoned.

"Well, these places are for losers; that's not how I see my son." His father looked around with a glare.

"You must take after your mother," said Trish. "You don't half make things hard for yourself."

Matt's face flushed bright red. "Shut up … just shut up! You have no right—"

"Come on, Trish." His father put the dog food in a carry basket. "You've upset him now. Let's get our dog food and go." They marched off to the checkout.

Rick rushed over and shot a vicious look at Matt. 'What have I told you about conversing with customers?"

"I can't help it," Matt said. "They were talking to me."

"That's as maybe. Now get back to work. We've got to finish the pet food and the toilet paper, and there are heaps of other aisles to be done."

"Well, I don't know if I can manage that on my own." ." Matt emptied the last of the pet food off his trolley onto the shelves.

"Just keep your mind on your work. If you don't want the job, there are plenty that do." He turned on his heel. Matt was glad when he saw that he was headed for the office upstairs.

Bloody hell, he needed the job, especially now they had rent to find every week on top of everything else. He wanted to tell Rick where he could stick his job but that wouldn't make his mother very happy or put food on the table. He didn't reckon he was cut out for this workaday shit. It was mindless and repetitive. It was nothing like surfboard shaping where your hands followed the contours of your board till they found the perfect shape.

Hell, he was simply filling an ever-sinking hole, and the money was just enough to keep him alive to do it. He never caught up. He was like a rat on a wheel chasing his tail. But there were always those who said he had a choice and he did. But get friggin' real, circumstances dictate. He had learnt that much in life.

He would go and see Kristy when he went out the back to refill, and see how Rick was treating her and if she could throw any girly wisdom his way. But then he saw her going up the stairs. The time had gone so quickly. It was the tea break. He followed her up and hoped not to see Rick. They wouldn't even get a break if he had his way.

He saw that Kristy was at the coffee machine when he went in. The rest of the workers were already seated and in their little cliques. The savoury smell of hot pies and fresh coffee filled his nostrils. The workers who had been there for years didn't associate with the newcomers like him and Kristy. They had to earn acceptance by seniority, otherwise the old hands treated them as if they were just passing through: barely worth getting to know. They sat around and gossiped about the latest workplace scandals or how terrible certain customers were.

He zeroed in on her

"It's good to get a break … been full on," Matt said.

"Tell me about it." Kristy stood at the coffee machine and stirred her coffee with a small stick.

She looked pretty with her blonde hair cascading to one side and her sea-green eyes shining out from under it. Her little black uniform stopped at the knee and nipped in wasp-like at the waist. Her sweetheart lips were in a nonchalant pout. He had an abhorrent vision of a Sidewinder's grease-stained hands groping her.

He sidled up and got a cup of tomato soup out of the machine. He took a sip. He burnt his top lip but it tasted rich and tomato-like, not at all like the usual instant soups. "This is good," he said.

"Coffee's not bad either," Kristy replied. She walked over to a table and sat down. She placed her coffee and egg sandwiches on the table in front of her. He pulled up a chair opposite and it scraped on the vinyl floor, making a noise that gained the attention of the other workers for a moment. He didn't think about picking any food up before work. He wasn't that hungry until now.

"Would you like a wholegrain egg sammy?" Kristy said.

"That'd be great." He slurped on his soup.

"Don't look so peeved. "

"Guess what?"

"What?"

"I ran into the Sidewinders up the Ramp."

"Those animals!"

"Yeah. Don't hang around Brighton on your own for a while."

'I wouldn't do that anyway."

"Well, be careful. I don't trust them."

"Me neither. They creep me out."

There was movement among the tables, lots of clatter of chairs and murmuring. People were starting to go back down to work, but Matt looked at the clock and they still had seven minutes to go.

Kristy began to wriggle in her seat. "Maybe we should think about going down."

"There's a good five minutes yet," Matt said.

"I know but Rick likes us to be on the floor a couple of minutes early, ready to go. "

"Well, tough," he said. "We're not paid for that."

Kristy got up, and he let her go.

He sat there reading about the latest employee of the month, an attractive young woman with short black hair and perfect teeth. That was one of the straws to clutch at on the journey to under-manager or branch manager or, for the high rollers, divisional manager: the top of a young employee's supermarket ambition. But no way, that wasn't for him or Kristy.

His concentration was broken by Rick's slinky frame blocking the cafeteria door. Rick strode over to his table and looked at his watch. "What's the meaning of this, Avery? Everybody else is at work."

"I'm on dinner break."

"Well, if you want to keep your job, get back to work — now!"

"I will; it's just about time."

"Because it's your first day, I'll overlook it."

Matt slowly got to his feet and dragged himself back to top up the toilet paper.

He guessed he would just have to ride it out and see how long Rick would put up with his behaviour. And how long he could handle working for a two-bit dictator. All he knew was, in the meantime, he had to keep on going.

SEVEN

MATT AND BJ cruised along in the Hilux past the old
Bowhill Road house. He scanned the street as they
passed. It brought home the reality of his situation:
deserted and left at the mercy of the marketplace. At
work they had reduced staff as a cost-cutting measure
and, if he was to keep his job, he was going to have to
do the work of two men to help his mother pay the rent.
He hated to see her struggle as a slushy cook. She was
not used to doing menial work and being barked at by
temperamental foul-mouthed chefs. The truck smelt of
spilt beer and stale cigarette smoke and the hood lining
was stained where water was getting in. They drove
past the new rental, which was a come-down from the
old house, light years away in terms of kudos. It was an
old holiday house, an orphan among the palatial homes
built on the ruins of houses like it. A new breed of young
executives who liked to be near the water to surf, kite
or paddle board had moved in with their Porsches and
BMWs.

The Hilux hummed along past the beachfront
properties on Marine Parade. Matt thought of his job
situation and it brought on a vision of Shelley's poem

The Mask of Anarchy. Just then they pulled in at the North Beach car park, and out of the blue he said:

"... What is Freedom? — ye can tell
That which slavery is, too well —
For its very name has grown
To an echo of your own."

"That's cool," said BJ. "Did you learn that from Kristy?" His brown eyes glistened and he opened the truck door.

"Yeah, and strangely enough the old man used to quote it when I was a kid."

"I bet he doesn't read poetry now," BJ said.

"Nah, he isn't human," Matt replied. He opened his door, slid out and began untying the boards. The onshore breeze tousled his hair, and he watched a nice little chest-high wave that was forming. The tide was about halfway in and the waves were still quite hollow despite the prevailing onshore wind. There were a few gulls shrieking at the shoreline and a handful of black forms bobbing around out the back.

"We should have got here earlier," Matt said.

"You're not wrong," BJ agreed.

A quick change, leg ties on and they paddled out. Matt recognised several people out the back — the Burrows brothers, Kobe, Jake, bully boy Edwards — and he got a big surprise to see Kristy. He paddled over to her with BJ in tow. She straddled her board with the nose sticking out of the water like a white pointer.

"I thought your folks had grounded you from surfing," Matt said with one eye on Kristy and one eye on the sets rolling in from further out the back. They looked like they might be getting bigger.

"They don't own me," Kristy said, positioning herself for a wave that was forming. She started to paddle frantically the way the boys had taught her. Matt and BJ paddled for the same wave and Matt yahooed as the ocean surged and the wave caught him. His body was in tune with the momentum beneath his board, but just at the last second he pulled out, knowing the wave was going to dump. He looked over and saw that BJ had pulled out too, but the inexperienced Kristy had gone over the falls with the wave and it dumped her violently into a churn of sandy white water. This was her first time out the back. After the wave subsided Kristy did not surface, but just as Matt and BJ were going to dive down and investigate, her head popped up in the dirty water.

"That was scary," she said, quivering and taking in big breaths of air. Her face was drained of colour and her hair was in straggles.

"You had us worried," Matt said. He stood in waist-deep water with his hand flat on his board.

"I've had enough for today," she said, and squinted with the sun in her eyes.

"Can we give you a ride?" Matt said.

"No, I'll text Mum; she's got the SUV."

"OK," Matt said. He flung his board around to

face out to sea, slid onto it and started to paddle."

BJ yelled at him. "Wait up, wage slave!" He followed Matt out the back. They sat in a huddle with Kobe and the crowd. The wind had come up and the waves were a bit irregular now, nothing for a while then several biggish ones in succession. Matt just let a medium one go but he watched as BJ and Jake Edwards took off on it. Edwards dropped in front of BJ and it is an unwritten law in surfing that if somebody drops in on you and threatens to take your wave, you push them off — and that's just what BJ did. Edwards hit the water with a shove from BJ, and he washed up in the inshore break and continued walking to shore with his board under one arm and a finger held high at BJ and the rest of the surfers out there.

The onshore wind was up and the waves began to deteriorate, what Matt knew as blown out, unrideable. He paddled into shore. He didn't want to freeze his arse off waiting for a half-decent wave that was never going to come. The others followed. They all headed to the sand dunes by the Memorial Hall, towelled off and dressed. They lounged on the dunes and Kobe divvied the joints out.

"I could get used to this," Matt said. "Beats the work ritual." He sucked in a big deep breath of smoke.

Ben Burrows exhaled a huge sweet-smelling cloud that curled above his head like a demented halo. "You'll have to come to one of our parties, bro. Plenty of skirt and this stuff. Even some meth if you want it."

"I'll stick to this," Matt said.

"That's what they all say," Kobe said, "but they soon want something with a more kick-ass buzz. Like coke. I can supply."

"Anything to take my mind off work." Matt took another toke"We get it," said Slade, the other Burrows brother. His black hair cascaded into his eyes.

"Anyway, guys, gotta go." He sucked a last long toke from the joint. "I start work at four."BJ collected their gear and boards, strapped them on the Hilux and they roared off to the new supermarket over by the estuary.

Matt always tried to get there early to have time to change into his uniform and to clock in. He jumped out of BJ's truck with five minutes to spare. His head was still buzzing from the weed, but he was in a good space to work. He raced up the side stairs and into the locker room to change. Before going downstairs, he checked himself in the mirror under the sign that read 'You never get a second chance to make a first impression.' He had to look good, because the customers were always there till eight-thirty. And it was always: "Hey you! Can you tell me where the vacuum cleaner bags and light bulbs are?" or "Do you have fuse wire?"

And he would have to explain ever so politely as far as fuse wire went that they were not a hardware store, and that the bags and bulbs were always in the most unlikely spot at the end of the beer and wine alley. He had been there long enough to know there was method in their madness and that products such as bread and milk were usually in the far-flung corners of the store so the customers would have to pass all the other items in the store to get to them. And that the high-turnover articles were stacked at eye level and the more slow moving items placed high above eye level or below. And that impulse buys were placed at checkouts where children could nag the parent into buying at the last minute if they didn't succumb themselves.

Rick was waiting for Matt at the bottom of the stairs, his black hair slicked back, and he was in his black store uniform. "Cutting it a bit fine, aren't you, Avery?" he said and looked at his watch. Bruce Springsteen was belting out 'Born in the USA' through the shop music system. Matt wondered if Rick wrote the play list. It occurred to him supermarkets were like casinos: they didn't have clocks. They didn't want to remind the customers how much time they were spending — or how much money, for that matter. It was all a bit of a game. They came in cars, flashed their plastic and left with a bootful of groceries, till next pay day.

Matt looked at his own watch. It was two minutes to four.

"I like my staff to be on the floor ten minutes early, ready to be briefed." Rick flicked through the pages on his clipboard. "Tonight you'll be starting on soft drinks and potato chips and when you finish that you can top up the household cleaners. I'll review the situation after that. I might get you to help the storeman."

"That's two guys' jobs," Matt said."

"Do you want to be one of them?"

"I guess."

Rick glared at him. "You don't sound very enthusiastic. Well, get on with it then. I'll check on you later. Remember, I want the stock rotated and anything past its use-by date goes."

"OK."

The flatdeck trolley Matt pushed seemed to have a life of its own. Three wheels worked fine but the fourth kept on twisting around, going every which way. He decided to take it out back, swap it over and fill up the new one with cartons of Coke. He passed the deli on the way; Rosemary waved and said "Hi" and Matt sucked in the aroma of freshly baked bread, which got his mouth going. He remembered he hadn't eaten since breakfast. He pushed his trolley out of the way of the customers and asked Rosemary for a big wedge of bacon and egg pie. She handed it to him after bagging and pricing it. He took it, rushed upstairs to get his eftpos card out of his jeans pocket and ran smack into Rick at the bottom of the stairs on the way back.

"What you are doing, Avery, away from your work area?"

"I just left my craft knife upstairs."

Rick looked at the pie in Matt's hand. "You know you are not supposed to purchase anything during your shift. One more incident like this and you'll be on a written warning. Seeing you already have it, I'll make an exception this time. Go pay for it. Then straight back to work, before I change my mind."

Matt ran to the self-serve machine, paid for his pie then went out the back to load up.

There were pallets everywhere. He had trouble getting through to the soft drink. He had just finished loading his trolley when Kristy came in to replenish her banana supply.

She waved Matt over. "Look at these," she said. "They are so green and when they ripen they taste like wood." And she showed him some apples. "These have been blast frozen and they are rotten in the middle."

"Have you told the boss?" Matt said.

"Yeah, he doesn't want to know," Kristy said, "as long as they look OK on the outside."

"Something has to be done."

"I've tried," Kristy said. "It goes against my nature ripping people off, but I need the job."

"We all do. And he knows it, the bastard. But he's not getting away with this. He's so careful about use-by dates on the other stock."

"I really don't like it," Kristy said. "He's also upping my workload. I feel like Shelley was on to it. I'm a glorified slave. I've had customers complain to me but they won't complain to him."

"We'll see about that." Matt curled his top lip. Yeah, what Rick was doing stunk. He'd beat the mongrel on this even if it cost his job.

EIGHT

MATT, BJ and Kristy sat in the Pier Restaurant encased in wraparound windows. It was cool to view the world through this glazed bubble and eat a steak. He couldn't afford to do it very often. He always liked to get a good table by the window with a view up the beach and watch the surfers catching a wave. This was usually only possible in the middle of the afternoon when there weren't many diners around. He loved the heady aroma of freshly brewed coffee. Kristy smelt of spring flowers, and she looked classic in her white muslin blouse and short denim skirt. The pity was she was only a salad girl.

The feeling of being cocooned in a glass bubble of the restaurant got Matt thinking about Coleridge's opium-fuelled vision and it just came out like it did sometimes:

"In Xanadu did Kubla Khan
A stately pleasure-dome decree:
Where Alph, the sacred river, ran
Through caverns measureless to man
Down to a sunless sea."

"The sun's shining on the beach," Kristy said and took another sip of her raspberry and Coke. "But I love that poem."

"It's thinly disguised porn," BJ said. "… pleasure-dome … deep romantic chasm … cedarn cover … fast thick pants … mighty fountain … forced … dancing rocks … the sacred river." BJ beamed. "We had it in English last year. The teacher tried to tell us it was describing Xanadu, the summer palace of the Mongol ruler and Emperor of China way back when. But I did some internet research."

Well, it didn't ring a bell for Matt. He wasn't in their gay English class.

"It conjures up all sorts of images," Matt said. "Maybe that's where the saying to get your rocks off comes from."

"It's called imagination," Kristy said.

"BJ's got a filthy mind." Matt laughed and flicked his glass with his forefinger; it made a dull ring. "It's all about being spontaneous, right, Kristy?"

"I guess it's what you want it to be, the individual response." Kristy blushed and looked at Matt.

"Way to go, Kristy," BJ said.

"Unfortunately, I can't sit here and discuss it." She moved in her seat. "I've got to work." Kristy slid her chair back and stood up.

BJ brushed his floppy fringe out of his big brown eyes. "Stuff work."

"Exactly," Matt said and he scratched his chin as if he had a goatee.

"I wish I could," she said. "Be good."

"We won't." BJ laughed.

"Catch you at work later." Matt gave her the hang loose sign.

As they watched her go, Matt whispered to BJ, "I hate to see you go, but I love to watch you leave."

"If Kristy knew what you were like, Avery, ..." BJ punched Matt lightly on the upper arm.

Matt punched him back in a playful way. "You reckon?" He scanned the few customers in the restaurant. He was glad Kristy had gone because he had an urgent scheme to hatch with BJ and he didn't want to disillusion her. After that big steak he felt like he could take on the world.

They sipped on what was left of their drinks and talked in hushed tones.

"I've got a job for us," Matt said.

"What sort of job?"

"It's payback for the old man ... gonna rip off his liquor cabinet."

"Isn't that a bit risky?"

"We'll be in and out."

"I don't know, Avery."

"You in? I'll do it with or without you."

"OK, but I'm not keen."

'We'll do it tomorrow. I'm not rostered on, and the old man told Mum they're on a property seminar for the weekend — up north."

Matt and BJ got up and walked out of the restaurant into the mellow air.

It was late afternoon the next day when Matt peered through the glass window in the back door of his father's new house. The burglar alarm wasn't turned on.

"He must be too busy making money to worry about protecting what he's got," Matt said.

BJ saw the alarm too. "That's a bit of luck," he said.

"Yeah," Matt said. "Let's go round the side and see if we can open a window."

"Sure." BJ followed Matt.

"Here," Matt said. "If I wiggle this window enough, I reckon the latch will spring." And with a little persuasion it did. "Give me a leg up, will ya? Then once I'm in I'll pull you through." BJ cupped his hands like a stirrup and heaved Matt inside in one sharp thrust. Matt landed with a thump on the shag pile carpet. He took in a lungful of air freshener and furniture polish.

"It's a palace," Matt said, still lying on the floor. He struggled to his feet with a dull pain in his backside from the fall. The house was a virtual antique shop showroom of sparkling glass and lacquered wood.

"Pull me up!" BJ yelled.

Matt opened the window wide, grabbed BJ by his flabby forearms and pulled. He came through the opening in one action, rolled onto the floor and clambered to his feet.

"Have a look behind the bar in the lounge. The grog's bound to be stashed there," Matt said. He breathed in short bursts with the full expectancy that his old man and his floozy might walk through the door at any moment.

BJ crept behind him. Matt could hear his urgent breathing too. "OK," BJ said.

Matt didn't know why they were creeping; if anyone was home they would have sussed them well before now. This was payback time. It wasn't stealing if you were taking from your old man; it was just a little overdue karma. "There's a couple dozen Heineken in the cartons," Matt said. "You grab those and I'll grab the bottles of Jack Daniel's and Coruba. The old man's staples."

"Sure thing," BJ said. His eyes darted and he listened for sounds of their arrival.

Matt whistled a little victory tune of his own making and stashed the bottles into plastic supermarket bags ready for the escape out the back door.

They loaded up the Hilux, which BJ had driven into the back yard. He spun the wheels in the gravel drive for a quick take-off. Matt looked behind and a little bald man with a huge handlebar moustache waved his fist at their retreat; they left him standing in their dust. Matt extended his middle finger out the passenger window and he choked on dust. So, they had an eyewitness and, when that neighbour passed on the description of the Hilux and the two young guys, his old man would soon do the maths.

The best thing now was to get rid of the evidence. They took the shortest route to North Beach. BJ pulled into a layby and parked under a wind-bent macrocarpa tree. They jumped out and Matt took a bottle of Coruba and one of Jack Daniel's from the back of the Hilux. BJ grabbed a carton of Heineken.

"Let's go up the dunes and party," Matt said. He thought some of the guys might be up there having a smoke or a drink. They carted the booze up the top of the dune and found a good spot out of the breeze with a wide view of the beach from Brighton to North Beach. They sat down.

Matt took a swig from the Jack Daniel's; it tasted like he imagined — high-octane fuel. He screwed up his face. The effect was immediate and it took the sharp edge off. The consequences of what he had just done seemed to melt away down his gullet and into his brain. He took another swig and retrieved a partly smoked joint from his plaid shirt pocket.

BJ lit him up with a throwaway lighter. He took a puff and passed it to BJ. None of the usual crowd was around. They had all this grog they would have to drink by themselves. He took another swig from the whiskey and just then a shadow passed between him and the sun. He held his hand up to shield himself and could make out the outline of an old tramp with bedraggled sun-bleached hair. He wore a full-length greatcoat, the type they sell in opportunity shops. As the tramp got closer, Matt got a whiff of a body that hadn't seen a shower for a while. But he was far enough gone to be extra friendly.

He held up the bottle of Coruba, which he didn't like anyway. "Want a drink, mister?"

The tramp sat down beside them. "Sure." He unbuttoned his coat so he could sit on the sand. "Randall Jones has never been known to turn down a drink. That's convivial, young fella."

"It's your lucky day," Matt said. He offered the old guy a puff of the joint.

"Never touch the stuff," he said. "This is my poison." He held the bottle up to his lips and glugged it down. "It's done me enough damage."

BJ finished the last of the joint and threw the butt on the sand.

Matt shifted into a reclining position and leaned on his elbow in preparation for a speech.

"I was married with two kids — a boy and a girl, both in their twenties now," the old guy said.

"And," BJ said.

"What?" Matt said.

"I had my own trucking firm, thirty trucks, fifty employees. To cut a long story short, I thought I could handle the booze ..."

They talked until they blotted out. Matt awoke early with the warm sun shining on his hungover head. It throbbed and ached. He squinted. The old man had gone. Events started to seep into his consciousness: the theft, the old man, the rum and whiskey gone too. Either they had drunk it last night or it went with him. At least they had cleaned up some of the evidence.

Matt shook BJ by the shoulder. "Hey! Wake up."

BJ stirred and shook his head. His eyes opened slowly. He looked around. "We must have got real wasted last night. Where's the old guy?"

"Gone," Matt said. "Our olds are going to be panicking."

"It's a wonder they didn't have the cops out looking for us," BJ said.

"I reckon." Matt knew he had a lot of consequences to face. Not only the stealing of the grog, but that he had let his mother down and worried her last night. His old man might not get the cops on him but he felt sure his fancy bit would.

NINE

MATT'S MOTHER sat at the computer desk. It was Sunday morning. Her head was down, as she concentrated on something as Matt opened the front door. The room had a smell of burnt toast. It stirred the juices in his gut. He hadn't eaten since last night, and wasn't looking forward to a row with her either. He was sorry for what had happened over the last twenty-four hours, but tough. It was a knee-jerk reaction to the way his father had treated him.

She got up from the desk and ambled over to the couch. She indicated for Matt to sit down opposite her. He wondered just how much his mother knew.

The phone rang and she got up to answer it. She waved at Matt to suggest he stay where he was. He could tell from what she said that his father was on the other end, and he was coming over soon.

She hung up and sat back down. "You can guess who that was. He's furious and, in this case, I can't say I blame him. How could you break into his house? And where were you the rest of the night? BJ's parents were frantic too, ringing around everybody."

Matt looked at the ragged, bold-patterned carpet. He

had it coming. "It's not stealing when you do it from your own family."

"Well, that's a peculiar view to take." She flashed her eyes at him. "I'm sure Trish won't see it that way." "That's just too bad. She doesn't count with me, anyway."

"Well, as it happens, it's more serious than that. You've broken the law, and if Trish wants to press charges, there's nothing your father or I can do. So I would be feeling a bit more charitable towards her if I were you."

"Whatever." He raised his head.

"That's foolish. It's time to grow up." She glared at him. "I was worried sick last night. I imagined the worst. It was your father who said not to get the police or I would have."

"I'm sorry. I didn't think."

She stood up. Her eyes calmed. "You must be famished. I'll make you some bacon and eggs."

"Not hungry." He ignored the rumblings in his stomach. He didn't want to hang around here any longer than he had to. She sat down again.

There was a knock on the door. It opened and Matt's father pushed through. His mouth was down at the ends and his eyes wide. "So you finally dared to show your face." He strode over to Matt and stood looking down on him. "I never thought my son would be reduced to the level of a common criminal."

"Must be in the genes." Matt's mouth turned into a perverse grin.

"Don't get smart with me. This is serious. It was all I could do to stop Trish calling the cops. You've let your mother and me down."

"Yeah, well, it's just a bit of payback. I'm sorry I upset Mum, but I don't care about you or your floozy."

"If you continue down this path, you will be beyond help from me or your mother." His father tried to get eye contact with him.

"Whatever … Is that it?"

"For now. Just be more sensible for all our sakes."

His father backed off. Matt stood up. "You mean like you? I'm gonna hit the beach. I need some fresh air."

"You've only just got home," his mother said.

"I know, but I promised Kristy."

His father sat on the couch that Matt had vacated. "Let's hope something will rub off."

Matt grabbed his board, which was leaning up against the house at the back door. He would have to walk. He had texted BJ, but he was grounded after last night. His parents weren't usually all that strict. He guessed staying out all night without letting them know bummed them out.

Kristy was in the surf when Matt got there. She was messing around in the inshore break. He watched as she waited for a decent wave then jumped on her board and paddled frantically. She was catching short rides right onto the beach. The waves were small and glassy. There were a few surfers out the back and a lot of fleshy mum and dad bathers with young kids. The sun sparkled on the rim of the waves as they crested.

There was a very slight offshore wind that held the face of the waves up. His mouth was dry after last night's boozing, and his stomach churned with hunger. He leaned his board against the sea wall, and then wandered down the road to get a pie and a Coke. Two bikers were sitting outside on their bikes, eating pies, as he approached the shop — Snake and Mullet.

"Hey, surfer boy." Snake waved him over to where they were parked. "We're worried about you, boy — hanging with that dude Kobe."

"He's a friend."

"Well, he's an enemy of the Sidewinders. I would hate for anything to happen to you or that little hottie of yours because of him."

"We go back a long way," Matt said.

"You've been warned," Snake said. "If you want weed, we got it."

"Maybe you ought to try a marketing campaign."

"Don't get smart with me. Now beat it before someone gets hurt."

Matt wandered in and bought his pie and Coke. They didn't scare him. They were all piss and wind. There were a lot of them — that was all. He was worried for Kristy, though. They wouldn't hold back with her. Hurting women was their thing.

He ripped the wrapper off the pie and took big

hungry bites. It was steak and cheese and just the right temperature. The monster in his stomach was happy now, washed down with the sting of cola. He was refuelled and ready to face the waves; his troubles already seemed like a distant memory.

He chucked the empty bottle into a roadside bin and took his T-shirt off. He wouldn't bother with a wetsuit today; he'd just wear the boardies he had on. There was no need to wax up, as there was plenty on the board from the last surf. He strolled to the water's edge and stuck his leg tie on. He would take Kristy for a session out the back. The waves were gentle enough to make the going out easy.

Matt waded out to where Kristy stood looking for a good wave. She didn't see him come up behind her. He tapped her on the shoulder. She spun around and a wave crashed on them both which held them under for a few moments. They came up gasping for air and grabbed their boards. Matt shuddered from the full blast of the wave on his upper body.

"Let's catch a few," Matt said.

"Sure, conditions are lovely." Her green eyes sparkled.

They turned their boards around, jumped on and paddled into the rolling waves. They had it pretty much to themselves. There were a few other surfers over towards Brighton, but Matt decided it would be best to keep their distance, especially as Kristy was still a newbie. A rogue wave poised to crash on them. He showed Kristy how to roll under it and plunge their way through. They were easy waves to do that on. Soon they were out the back straddling their boards, rising and falling with the sea as though it had a heartbeat and rhythm all of its own. The morning sun warmed his shoulders and soothed the back of his neck.

The waves lapped at their boards. "My olds are getting a bit strange," Kristy said. She scanned the horizon for a good set.

"I noticed." Matt twisted his board around with his hips to face an approaching wave. "Here's a good one … start paddling." The ocean rose up beneath them. The waves had picked up in size. He looked over in front of him to see Kristy paddling for all she was worth. The wave caught them both. At the last minute he pulled back. He watched Kristy slide down and across from behind. Then she screamed. Her board shot into the air and she disappeared in the white water. But she soon surfaced; the waves didn't have much power.

Matt paddled over to where she went down.

Her head broke the surging surface. He sat up on his board. "Not bad for a start."

He slid off his board into the water beside her. "What did you mean about your parents?"

Another wave threatened to break on them. They punched their heads through it and came out in the trough behind it.

"It's Dad. He doesn't think I should hang with you guys."

"What do you think?" They rose up the face of another wave about to break on them.

"I think he's a snob. I'll see who I want."

They stood in water up to Kristy's chest, dodging the waves. Matt had the sudden urge to hold her. They both let their boards float to the ends of the ties. What the hell. He would follow his feelings. He put his hands on her shoulders, drew her towards him and kissed her. It was a long, lingering kiss. He supported her shoulders in the water, and she clung to him with her hands around his neck.

A wave crashed over them and broke the clench. Their boards bobbed overhead.

Matt surfaced at the same time as Kristy. A warm sensation filled his chest and moved to his head. Two lines from *Kubla Khan* spun around in his brain like a spinning top. Kristy pulled the string. He placed one hand on her bony shoulder and with the other lifted the golden strands of hair out of her eyes. He spoke slowly and with emphasis:

"For he on honey-dew hath fed,
And drunk the milk of Paradise."

"That's so beautiful," Kristy said."It's how I feel," Matt said.

"One day you will use your own words."

"I can't imagine it."

"I can," Kristy said. The waves had picked up now, and the wind flicked spray off the tops into their faces.

"Promise me one thing," Matt said.

Kristy brushed hair out of her eyes. The salt water and sun had turned it into straggles.

"What?" she said.

"Keep well away from the Sidewinders. They might try to hurt you again." He bounced over a wave. She looked directly into his soft blue eyes. "Don't worry. They really creep me out. You stay away from them too."

"You got it … It sucks that we have to work tonight."

"It sure does."

Matt's skin was beginning to look like prunes. It had that wrinkly look you get from lying in a bath too long, except he had goose bumps as well. It was definitely too cold for board shorts, especially if you were going to spend hours in the surf.

He could take the cold or heat now. It was the way his old Science teacher Locke had explained the Theory of Relativity to the class. He didn't notice if he was freezing his arse off or burning up. It was all relative because Kristy's hotness put all else into the background. But maybe that simplified the profound too much. But, what the hell? He still had to go to work tonight to keep the money rolling in. And he didn't know how long he could keep it up.

TEN

A SIREN wailed. By the time Matt saw the blue and red flashing lights they were nearly at the supermarket, so BJ drove into the car park. The police wagon followed, and BJ pulled into a park right at the front of the shop. The police parked beside him.

"I wonder what's up," Kristy said.

Two officers got out of their vehicle. One was clean shaven, and the other one had a thin black moustache. The one with the moustache tapped on BJ's window. He wound it down.

The Alsatian police dog barked a deep and sinister bark.

"Step out of the vehicle, please," the officer said. "I'm Senior Constable Tony Sykes. This is Constable Wilson." Wilson checked BJ's registration. It was up to date.

"We have reason to believe you have drugs in your possession," Sykes said. Wilson let the dog out of the wagon and put it on a lead. "Now line up over here and let the dog sniff you."

"Have you got a warrant?" Kristy said.

"We don't need one when we suspect you have class A drugs in your possession," Sykes said.

"What made you believe we have drugs?" Matt said.

"We don't reveal our sources," Sykes said.

"You all seem to be clean. Now I'm going to put the dog in the car." The dog indicated at a butt on the floor. "Aha!" Sykes said. "So you have been smoking in here. We are not going to prosecute over that, but you've been forewarned. We have our eye on you."

Wilson put the dog in the back of the wagon. They climbed in the front and drove away.

In the meantime a crowd had gathered from the car park. The checkout operators and supervisors had been craning their necks out the window between customers. This was something Matt didn't need on top of everything else, especially with Rick.

BJ took off in the Hilux and left them standing there.

Rick was waiting at the entrance as they came in. "All right, you two, in my office — now!"

Matt and Kristy followed Rick up the stairs. The blood pumped in Matt's veins. Bloody hell, how was he going to explain this? Now even Kristy had been implicated. He sure didn't want that. She never touched drugs and wouldn't approve of him using. He wondered briefly if it was the Sidewinders, but he realised they would never resort to the cops. Nah, it wouldn't be them. The thing is, would this stuff up his job?

Rick was sitting in his high-backed chair when they entered his office.

"OK, come in and sit down." He pointed to two leather tub chairs.

They sat down in front of him.

"Well, I don't think I have to tell you it's not a good look for employees of Food World to be frisked by the police for suspicion of possession of drugs in full view of our customers."

"That's all it is," said Matt, "suspicion. We are not guilty of anything, especially Kristy. She's never ever touched drugs."

"What are you saying ... you have?"

"Well, only outside of work."

"You've got me wondering now if I should drug test you."

"I'm clean," Matt said. "And Kristy never touches the stuff."

"I can speak for myself," Kristy said. "I flatly deny anything to do with drugs. Not that it is any of your business. I won't stand for attacks on my good name."

"Well, what concerns me is your performance here. This is not a good look for any of us. And it casts aspersions on our other staff. Any more trouble from either of you and you will be on a written warning. Now get back to work before I change my mind."

Matt left Rick's office with a dry sensation in his throat. He had lost that certain lightness in his step. He was responsible for what happened to Kristy. Shit! He had drawn the police to her and BJ. The question that remained was who tried to set him up? And for sure he would find out.

He walked out of the office and caught Kristy's angry stare. "I hope this doesn't mean we are over."

"No, it doesn't," she said. There was a hint of tears. "But if my father ever finds out, it will give him something extra to diss you with."

"Are you going to be at the beach tomorrow?"

"Sure. If I can get away."

"OK, I'll catch ya then."

The rest of the night for Matt was one big blur of frantically stacking shelves, and tidying up the empty cartons and rubbish out in the loading bay. But, hey, he didn't want to upset Rick too much or he might be down the road. He just got on with his work and thought about Kristy and surfing — in that order.

Matt and BJ pulled into the North Beach car park. The early-morning sun scorched his face and chest through the truck window and warmed him right through. They got out of the truck and found the gap in the beach wall. They spotted Kristy backed into the wall on the beach side. Wow! She looked sexy: far hotter than he could have hoped for. That skimpy bikini barely covered anything. Hard to believe she was his girl.

She languished on a giant beach towel with the signs of the zodiac on it. They cleared some driftwood out of the way and sat on the fine white sand either side of her. Matt turned over on his stomach and rested his hands under his chin so he could talk to her close up. The hot sand caressed his whole body as he wriggled down into a comfortable position.

"Do you believe in that horoscope stuff?" Matt said.

Kristy sat up on her haunches. "Mum gave it to me, but I'm a bit sceptical. It's all very unscientific."

"It's bullshit," BJ said. "How can rocks influence people?"

"Well, that I don't know, but it intrigues me. Like, I'm a Libra and I like balancing things up and rescuing people."

"That could apply to half the human race," BJ said.

Matt looked at them both. "I read this thing once. It was about how planets might give off very subtle rays, which act like transmitters, and we act like receivers, you know, TV sets."

"Sounds like a science fiction novel, or Hinduism," BJ said.

"I don't know," Kristy said. She put her head on the side like a puppy. "Might be true."

There was a low rumble of big bikes. Matt felt it in his guts. He jumped up and looked over the wall as Mullet and a young gang prospect pulled up. He could tell he was a prospect because he didn't wear a gang patch. He still had to earn it by breaking the law, or taking the rap for one of the more senior bikers. It was the same biker that had pawed Kristy. He was tall and wiry, and he had heard them call him Stretch.

The bikers straddled their bikes in front of the wall.

"Nice to see you again," Mullet said. "Keeping out of trouble?"

"I never do anything else," Matt said." How 'bout you guys?"

Stretch slid off his bike. He sauntered over through the gap to where they lay. He moved in closer and bent over Kristy. "Now if I had a bit of this …" He lifted a strand of hair off Kristy's face. "… things might be different."

"Back off," Matt said. "Didn't you learn anything last time?" He sprang to his feet.

"Yeah, piss off," BJ yelled.

"Let the lady decide," Stretch said.

"Please go away," Kristy said. "We don't want any trouble."

"For now," Stretch said. "You'll keep." He stood up and backed off. "A woman doesn't always mean what she says. I'll be back to collect." He swaggered back to his bike. It burst into a low but throaty rumble, as if it had been modified.

Kristy trembled. "I meant what I said."

Matt watched Mullet and Stretch disappear down Bowhill Road. The blood built in his veins. It was worse than he feared; not only did he have his own problems to sort out, but he had to worry about Kristy. How would he keep her out of the clutches of the Sidewinders? Going to the cops was no good because the Sidewinders would just deny everything. And it would give them another reason to get back at them. He reckoned the best thing was to get Kristy home. His appetite for surfing had gone for the day.

Matt put his arm around Kristy.

"Have I missed something between you two?" BJ said.

"I'm just worried for her. I think it's best if we quit for the day."

"And I'm not? OK, I'll drop you both off."

"Thanks." Kristy rubbed her eyes.

"You can drop me at the surf shop." Matt let his arm fall from Kristy's shoulder. "I want to catch up with Jack."

"All right, the surf's not that great, anyway. I'll go and play some Grand Theft Auto."

"Whatever," Matt said.

The front door of the surf shop was locked when he arrived. Matt put his hand up to the glass and could see that the light was on in Jack's office at the back of the shop. He knocked on the window but there was no answer. He banged a bit harder, and he could see Jack's lean frame moving towards him to unsnib the door. The mall was quiet and Jack's shop had been tagged since his last visit.

He opened it. "You're keen," he said. "Eager to get working on that blank?"

"Yeah, the surf's crap."

"Come into my office and we will have a talk about what sort of board you want to create."

Matt's heart thumped in his chest, and board designs spun in his head. What sort of board would he make? Wow, he was finally going to get the chance to build the board of his dreams. Jack was going to help him do that.

Jack's office was larger than it looked from out in the shop. The walls were lined with posters of boards over the years. Above his desk was a framed black and white picture of Duke Kahanamoku surfing in Hawaii on one of his wooden long boards, and others of him when he visited New Brighton. There was also a framed article about the Duke being a five-time Olympic medallist in swimming. Cool, he had no idea about that. There was also a rogue's gallery of the world's most famous surfers. He recognised most of the faces. A surfing magazine lay on Jack's desk featuring the world's top ten shapers.

A computer with a large screen filled the desk space. Jack motioned Matt to sit in one of several wooden Cape Cod deck chairs.

Matt sat down.

"Are you comfortable?" Jack said.

"Yeah. I feel as though I'm at the beach."

"Good, that's the general idea." Matt cast an eye over a poster with a montage of classic waves in different stages of breaking.

"Now." Jack shifted in his seat. "Before you get bogged down with design theory, it's good to keep it simple for your first few boards."

"Whaddya mean?" Matt said.

"I suggest a shape with clean lines. Forget extreme curves in rocker or outline for your first board."

"I'd go with that," Matt said.

"If you muck up a small wave board it's not as bad as ruining a trendy Mavericks gun."

"I'll keep that in mind."

"Most beginner shapers go for a small-wave design for their first board, because they are simple shapes, flat and wide."

"I reckon that's good advice."

"Well, it comes from years of trial and error. Don't go for a triple-wing swallow Bonzer first up."

Matt cast his eyes over the surfing memorabilia on the walls and floors of Jack's office. He picked up an ornament of an old school long board from Jack's desk and ran his forefinger over its lacquered finish. He knew this was what he wanted to do with his life. His decision was made sweeter in knowing it was a career path his father didn't want for him. But it was bitter because he needed money to stick it to his father. For now this job wasn't going to provide it. And he suddenly remembered he had an appointment with his old man and Trish tomorrow because his mother wanted him to make things good for stealing the booze. Like that was gonna work.

ELEVEN

TRISH OPENED the door to Matt.

"I've come to apologise to both you and Dad for the break-in."

She was matter-of-fact. "You had better come in then. Your father's at the table." Matt went through to the kitchen and stood beside his father who was reading the morning paper.

His father looked up. "Hello, stranger, it's good to see you."

"He has something he wants to say to us both," said Trish busily clearing up.

Matt watched Trish as she strutted between the kitchen table and the dishwasher in their palatial Parklands home. She obviously thought she was oh so sexy from her short spiky platinum hair to the tips of her red pumps. Her neck and hands dripped with chunky gold and diamond jewellery. She was a living breathing package of everything his father stood for. He guessed she made his old man feel good — or at least young again. Not like when his father looked at his mother and cringed. Did she remind him of how old he had grown too?

Matt didn't want to be there. It was only on his mother's insistence that he apologise for the break-in. The surroundings made him nervous; the shag pile carpet, shiny antiques and trendy art that clung to the mushroom-coloured walls had Trish's signature all over them. Her strong perfume mixed with the furniture polish, creating a heady whiff that filled his nostrils as she whooshed past him. He shouldn't have been there.

Trish stopped what she was doing and pulled up a chair opposite Matt and his father. His father put his newspaper down. All was quiet.

Matt took a deep breath. "I would just like to say," he cleared his throat and looked down, "that I'm very sorry for breaking in and stealing your liquor."

"Well, I won't pretend I wasn't extremely disappointed in you and your friend. But we were all young and impetuous once." He looked sheepishly in Trish's direction. "It says something that you have manned up."

Matt offered them the change he had in his pocket, which amounted to twenty-odd dollars. "Maybe this will help towards it."

"Keep your money," his father said. "I know it's been earned the hard way. If you want to make amends just ensure nothing like this ever happens again. Now that's an end to it."

Trish didn't look so sure, but she took the opportunity

to change the subject. "I had an email from Liam yesterday," she said.

"Really?"

"He's coming home, and he would like to work for us."

"Oh, that's good." His father's voice fell flat.

"Don't sound so excited." She stuck her chin out. "I'm sure you would feel differently if it were Matt."

"No, I wouldn't," his father said.

"Don't mind me," Matt said, "just talk about me as if I wasn't here." He flushed red.

His father went back to his newspaper. There was an awkward silence. Trish slipped out of her chair to fidget in the kitchen, reorganising the already immaculate pantry. It occurred to Matt that his father might not have left home if he knew he was going to build an empire and leave it all to another woman's son.

Hang on, hang on — maybe this was just a trick to make him keen. But, tough, it just made him determined to stay out of it. His father would go along with Trish for now, and she would have to go along with him later. But, as for him, not interested. It wasn't going to happen. He was going to be a board shaper.

Matt got up to leave.

"Where are you going?" his father said.

"I'm going to work on my board at Jack Dawson's."

"I didn't know you knew Jack. We are old surf buddies. Remember me to him."

Trish turned around from the pantry. "You going so soon? Sure you won't stay for a drink?"

Her voice dripped sarcasm.

"Come on, give him a break. His bad behaviour is in the past," his father snapped.

"I don't know about that," Trish said.

'Well," his father said, "I think we should let it drop. It was a plain stupid thing to do, but I'm over it."

Matt's eyes flared. "So getting pulled over by the cops and frisked for drugs had nothing to do with this."

"Of course not. We wouldn't be likely to make it a police matter, would we, Trish?" his father said.

Trish's brow wrinkled. "I didn't prosecute, but I couldn't let them off the hook completely. I tipped off a cop friend of mine to keep an eye on them."

"Thanks!" Matt stiffened. "Thanks for everything." He spun on his heel and stomped out.

His father's mouth dropped but he said nothing.

Jack Dawson was huddled over the computer in his office when Matt slipped through the door. Dawson looked up from a radical board design on the screen as Matt pulled up a beach chair and looked on. He caught a faint smell of fibreglass from the glassing bays. This was becoming his world, surrounded by all this cool surfing stuff. It was the one place the crap in his head stopped and everything made sense. "I checked out the surf on the way over," Matt said. "It was small."

"I know," Dawson said. "I was going to go out myself. I ran through a few designs for your first board. I think something around two metres with a thick nose, low rocker, maybe a pintail with the fins well back — good for surfing small, mushy waves but also easy for bigger, steeper days."

"Yeah, that's really cool. When do I start?"

"Soon. I've just got to finish off here. Then we will go and pick you out a polystyrene blank."

"That's a gnarly board you're looking at now."

"Yeah, it's a gun for a special big wave surfer client."

They got up to leave the office and the rumble hit them like a small earthquake. Through the window in the front of the shop Matt could see the Sidewinders riding in a close formation, and he could smell their exhausts.

"They never grow up," Dawson said. "Snake is as old as I am. He's still hanging like a teenager."

"You know him?" Matt said.

"Yeah, we've got history. Snake, I knew him as Billy Brice in those days. Believe it or not he was a champion surfer. He always had a bike. He had a special rack made so he could carry his board on it."

"What happened?"

"He got jilted at the altar."

"For real?"

"Yeah. He was all set to settle down for the whole catastrophe: marriage, mortgage, kids. It all went to custard. She left him for another guy: a hotshot young lawyer."

"That explains a lot."

"Yeah, but a word of advice: stay away from him. I don't know what he and that gang of his are into these days but they are violent and dangerous. He doesn't like surfers. His girlfriend was a surfer, lifesaver and law student."

"Wow!"

"Yeah, he's got it in for surfers, and he has never surfed since the break-up."

"Well, I wasn't expecting that."

"Yeah, well, let's concentrate on the matter at hand. First, we must sort out a blank."

They walked through into the factory area. Dawson flicked through a pile of foam blanks in a bin and chose one the right length and thickness. He placed it onto the rack. "This should do the trick."

"That one looks good," Matt said.

They both stood back and admired it sitting on the rack.

"Before you do anything else you are going to have to take the dimensions and make up a template. We have to take your weight and height into consideration." Dawson showed him one cut out of cardboard for a big wave board. "I think we might leave that till next time. You don't want to run before you can walk."

"Sounds good to me and, anyway, I have to meet friends at the beach soon."

"Have a quick clean-up of the vacant bays and I'll drop you off. I have to go soon too. Remember, shaping's all about creative use of the eyes, hands and imagination."

"That's cool; I'll go and clean. Thanks for all your help." It didn't take him long to do, and Jack dropped him at the beach.

BJ and Kristy were sitting in the Hilux when Dawson dropped Matt at North Beach. Matt pulled the back door open and slid in behind them. Kristy's sweet floral scent hit him hard as it wafted around the cab, and it turned him on. The weather had spun round to the southwest. It was cooling down fast and the surf was deteriorating.

"I reckon we should try it over at Sumner. It's always good there when the surf's crap here," BJ said.

"Good idea," Kristy said. "I'm ready for a surf anywhere."

"It's not gonna get any better here on this tide," Matt said.

BJ fired the diesel up and it rattled away like a tired old taxi. They all retreated into their thoughts. Matt mulled over what Jack Dawson had said about Snake. He looked over Kristy and BJ's shoulders as they followed the dunes through South Brighton, and then joined the estuary bordered by the sewage settling ponds. He heard the rumble of the Sidewinders as they flanked the Hilux, forming a creepy escort.

"I don't like this," BJ said.

"Neither do I," Kristy replied.

"Don't worry," Matt said. "Snake's got a thing about surfers, that's all."

"That's really comforting," BJ said. He veered left for them to overtake. They soon accelerated past, one deep *burr ... oom* at a time. Matt looked at the road as they turned left by his supermarket and followed the causeway and the bikers all the way to where the estuary met the sea at Sumner, which lay in a basin of hills and faced Pegasus Bay and the Pacific Ocean.

Matt had been windsurfing with his father on this estuary, and he had showed him the abundant bird life on and around the spit and adjacent wetlands: the shags, oystercatchers, stilts and especially the godwits that migrate and return, which is a local event. The Sidewinders stayed ahead of them. But they didn't do anything, just freaked them out.

The traffic bottlenecked near Shag Rock, where shipping containers were still in place at the bottom of the cliffs to prevent falling rocks from hitting the road below. Matt liked Sumner, a very upmarket beach suburb fronted by opulent houses, apartments and a scattering of cafés, restaurants, boutiques and a movie theatre.

He watched as a crowd of people enjoyed the balmy weather, while the bikers idled through them as if they were sheep.

He knew Sumner had really boomed in the last fifteen years despite devastating damage from the quakes. Three people had been killed here. The quakes hit

Clifton Hill especially hard; it still looked dodgy, with occasional landslides. At one stage a house had fallen over the edge. And further around, the RSA had been squashed flat by a gigantic rock.

As a kid he had played on top of Cave Rock, a volcanic outcrop that separated the surf beach, Scarborough, from the swim beach. And he had chased BJ through its caverns.

The bikers had pulled into a beach-front café.

He liked to walk the beach to Shag Rock, another volcanic outcrop, at the mouth of the estuary. It was now half its former size thanks to the quakes. And walking back the roadway he would marvel at the cave under the cliffs where they had once found moa bones.

They headed to Scarborough with its small park, kids pool, café and clock tower. Over the hill was Taylors Mistake, another great surf beach.

BJ did several passes before he could get a park. The east end of the beach was hidden by a stone wall, so they all got out and stepped through a break in the wall. This part of the beach called Scarborough was about a kilometre long.

Matt shielded the sun from his eyes and watched as regular shoulder-height waves rolled in. It was a real contrast to what was happening at North Beach. BJ stood beside him and pulled the peak of his baseball cap down. "I told you it would be good." The sky was overcast and churning.

"I've never surfed anything this big," Kristy said with a catch in her voice. Blonde strands of hair hung in her eyes, and she backed into the stone wall.

"It's not so big," Matt said. "They are quite tame." He scratched his chin. "They aren't dumping. It will be easy to get out."

"I'm just a bit nervous, that's all."

Matt put his arm round her. "We'll watch you. You'll be fine."

"Get a room," BJ said.

In a flash they were in their wetsuits and paddling out. There was a bit of a rip on and Matt knew that they had to let the rip take them out. There were two main rips on this beach, one at each end. Then once out they would have to paddle west parallel to the beach to get free of it. He and BJ had already done just that. But Kristy didn't follow them. She was in trouble. She paddled frantically for shore but the rip was just taking her sideways to the jetty and the rocks on Whitewash Heads.

Shit! Kristy was in deep doo-doo; the rip had her in its grip and she was helpless against it. He paddled frantically towards her. The ocean moved under them like a fast-flowing river. Another few minutes and she would be on the rocks.

"Help me, Matt, help, please … it's got me," she screamed.

Matt paddled up alongside her. "Don't panic! Start paddling out to sea and then level with the beach.

You're fighting it and getting in deeper. Follow me." He paddled with firm even strokes, and took in big gulps of air. He began to think it was too late because Kristy was paddling with everything she had and they were standing still. But then he saw they were moving up the beach: he could tell because he lined them up with a house on the shore, and they moved ahead of it.

BJ paddled over to them, but by then they were coming out of it.

"I think we better go in," Matt said.

"That's not silly," BJ said.

Kristy shivered. "I was terrified. I think I've got a lot to learn."

"It happens to us all. That was your first lesson on rips," Matt said.

Back on the beach they put their boards down and sat on a bench seat overlooking the whole of Scarborough Beach. They had just towelled off when Kobe poked his head through the gap in the wall and bully boy Edwards was with him, but when Edwards saw Matt he disappeared back through the gap.

"I thought that was your truck," Kobe said. "Want some smoke?"

"Not just now." Matt looked at Kristy and dropped his gaze. He had to play the innocent and didn't want to encourage Kristy into smoking. If her olds found out, that would be the end of their relationship. Her father would see to that.

"I'd like a puff," Kristy said. "It might settle me."

"I might give it a miss. I've got to do a shift tonight, and so do you," Matt said.

That was all he needed — Kristy smoking dope. It had been a big day. He still had a lot of unanswered questions in his mind, but his main concern was how long he could keep the money rolling in. And he was also worried about Kristy. In Snake's twisted mind, hurting her would be getting back at the woman who deserted him. It wouldn't pay to let Kristy out of his sight. The bikers were following them and always seemed to know where to find them. The ugly truth was becoming clearer by the day: it was Kristy they wanted.

TWELVE

"HOW DID the visit to your father go? Did you apologise for the break-in?" his mother shouted as he came through the front door.

Matt walked on over to an armchair beside the couch she was sitting on. He sat down. "No way! You couldn't wait, could you? I bet the next questions are what did she look like? And has she put on any weight?"

His mother crossed her legs. "I was just showing interest in your visit, that's all." Her face reddened.

"I'm sorry, Mum. I guess I just overreacted. She's the same old middle-aged tart and he hasn't changed: still trying to get me to abandon you the way he did."

"Now that's overreacting — and it's disrespectful to her and your father."

"It's the truth though."

"It might be, but it doesn't help anybody." She blinked. "Anyway, we have to concentrate on our life. How's your job going?"

Matt lay back in his chair with his arms behind his head. His mother had a roast on. The smells were putting his stomach through somersaults. He wondered, should he tell her he might not be working at the supermarket much longer, or should he hit her with the truth about what a prick Rick was? He didn't want to let his mother down. She was old school and sucked up to those in power as if they had a sort of divine right to lord it over others.

She thought of them as being better than the average wage slave, though she would never call them that. Rick would be one of them. Workers should know their place and respect the powers that be: a very uncool idea. No prizes for what his mother would think of a board shaper. She had respect for those that were in trades and worked with their hands but they were ordinary. She was terrified he would end up ordinary — or worse, unemployed, a no-hoper. He decided to keep his thoughts to himself. "Work's good."

"Dinner will be ready in a minute."

"Good, I'm starved."

She stood up. "Go and have a quick shower and I'll get it ready."

He showered and changed in about five minutes flat and came back all fresh and warm. His roast lamb and veges were on the table, so he sat down and got straight into it.

"This is top stuff. I bet she doesn't cook like this."

It was the highest compliment he could have paid his mother. He could tell when she looked up, beaming. "Thank you, dear, it's nice to be appreciated."

That's what he was going to a shit job for — a home-cooked meal like that. "Well, I appreciate you. Not just for the lovely meals — for everything."

"Well, that is nice."

"One little thing, Mum. Can you drop me at work? BJ was going to, but he had to go out with his olds."

"I've got to do a shift, dear. Sorry."

"OK, I'll take my bike."

At the supermarket he saw that a police car was parked near the entrance, and two policemen talked to a cluster of teenage girls in school uniform. It was as if the whole school had descended on the place; their backpacks cluttered the entranceway and the area that housed the trolleys. There had been a big interschool rugby tournament that day.

It was the same policemen who had cautioned them before. One of the officers spoke to Matt as he was about to walk past. "So, Mr Avery, I see you didn't heed our warning."

"About what?" Matt said, leaning on his bike.

"Our beach patrols have noticed you with a known drug offender, one Kobe Jacobs."

"He's a friend from the beach."

"A word to the wise: if he goes down, you don't want to be one of those that goes with him and blemish what is, up until now, a completely clean record. Think of the inconveniences that might cause with jobs and travel and life in general. That would be a sad day."

He scribbled in a notebook.

Matt kept on walking. "No need to worry on that score. I'm into surfing, not drugs. Gotta go. I'm already late for work."

"It may not be a warning next time." The officer went back to interviewing the girls.

Matt put his bike in the rack in the car park.

Rick was waiting the other side of the entranceway. He looked at his watch. "It's eight minutes past four. You're late again, Avery. If I can get here on time, I don't see why you can't."

"I was, but the cops stopped me outside."

"Well, if you stayed the right side of the law it wouldn't happen. Now get down into the toiletry aisle. It's a mess. Boxes and trolleys are all over the place. The last shift left it like that. Finish off the stacking and clean up."

"They are short-staffed."

"I'm in charge here. You do your job and I'll take care of mine. Now get to it."

It was the old boss–worker thing alive and well and it made Matt churn inside with hate and anger.

He couldn't work it out. Teachers had waffled on at school about technology, and how technology was going to work for us, be a tool. We should all be sitting back watching it work by now. What went wrong? And Tiny Jones sprang to mind, his Social Studies teacher. He used to talk to the kids about bosses and workers. It didn't mean shit to most of them. It wasn't supposed to be on the curriculum. The other teachers called him a dinosaur. Matt learned from him that working conditions were going backwards, but it didn't figure until now.

He didn't fully get it: the days of unions and what they did for workers. He would quiz Jack Dawson about it sometime; he had come through the old school.

Rick wasn't really an employer, but he sucked up to them by saving his bosses money. He had their mindset, and was what his mother would call a ne'er-do-well. At times like this, Matt's dreams kept him going, and flashed like neon in his mind. Maybe it was dreams that kept everybody going, whether they were going to be a divisional manager or a board shaper.

Yes, it was dreams that kept us going. Even a garbage man could have Hollywood dreams, and he had once heard someone say real dreams couldn't be destroyed. It was comforting. It made him warm inside when Rick gave him a hard time. It made the idea of being a successful board shaper seem real.

It didn't take him long to finish the toiletry aisle, but then he had a couple of displays to do. He was just finishing the last aisle of the night when Rick crept up beside him.

"Well done," Rick said. "You did two men's work tonight." His lips curled in a slimy grin.

Matt's hands clenched and his breathing came in short bursts. He just wanted to hit out at anything that moved or got in his way, but years of martial arts had taught him self-control. It was all he could do to hold back the fight or flight response, one of the most basic human responses, another lesson from Tiny. He had to keep on telling himself not to react with his fists — to run was the better option. The blood rose in his body like a tide of hatred. He pulled out everything to stop from drowning in it.

But he somehow kept a lid on it. It was the same feeling he had when his father told him he was leaving for another woman. He doubted he would get over it in a hurry. But he was glad it was the weekend and he would be able to wash away all the shit in the surf. It was a real bummer but there were a lot of cool things happening in his life, namely Kristy and Jack Dawson, but he would not see them tomorrow. Jack was out of town and Kristy was having a big family reunion. It would be good to catch up with BJ. The short breaths had evened out, and the pulsing blood settled in his veins as he rode home on his faithful bike.

Most mornings meant surfing. He arrived at North Beach at 9 a.m., and just in time, it seemed. Bully boy Edwards had BJ by the collar of his Hawaiian shirt. The rest of the beach-goers walked past with frowns on their faces or looked the other way. BJ was frozen. What had happened to all the martial arts training he had given him? He had shown BJ how to break that sort of grip.

But he had just frozen in fear.

He tapped Edwards on the shoulder.

Edwards turned around. "This is between us, Avery." He bared his teeth like an angry dog.

Matt got him in a headlock and he soon let go of BJ. "I told you before: you mess with my friends, you've got a fight with me." "He said I was gay."

"Well, what's new about that?" Matt said.

"It's lies."

"Whatever, but if you mess with BJ again, you'll be talking in a high-pitched voice, understand?"

Matt tightened his grip.

"I un … der … stand."

When he let Edwards go, he ran off over the road and kept on going without looking back.

"Thanks, buddy," BJ said.

"No problem. How about you use what I taught you next time?" He flexed his shoulders.

"I would've. He just scared me, that's all."

"OK, let's forget it. Your olds let you off the hook?"

"Yeah, we're all sweet now. Do you wanna go for a surf?"

"Maybe later. It'll be bigger on the full tide." They walked around the side of the Memorial Hall onto the beach and leaned with their backs to the dunes overlooking the surf. A figure approached from down the beach. He had a familiar swagger about him.

"Hey, that's Kobe," BJ said.

"Yeah, it's unusual to see him on foot." He had a beach bag over his shoulder and, once he spotted them, he came over. He sat down in front of them on the sand, and they joined him.

"What are you doing on the beach?' Matt said.

"I'm just doing my rounds out of sight of bikers and prowl cars. Want a smoke?"

"I do but we've been sort of warned off you. Let's go higher up the dunes."

They climbed up the embedded wooden steps that led from the beach entrance, and it took them deep into the interior of the sand dunes. They sat on a high point where they had a view of the road to the west and the beach to the east. They could see anybody before they approached, and they were hidden by tall marram grass.

Kobe took two foil-wrapped packages out of his bag. They looked like silver cigars. He handed them one each. "That's twenty bucks a throw."

"Put it on our tab. How much we owe you?" Matt said.

"It's sixty bucks a piece, so far. How's the job going?" Kobe asked.

"Only just," Matt said. "I'm going to walk out or they are going to fire me, whichever comes first."

"Sorry to hear that, but I'll be looking for a couple of guys soon to do a bit of harvesting."

"I don't think we could risk it. The cops are already watching us."

"The job's not local. You'd be well clear."

"We're not that desperate, are we, BJ?"

"No way," BJ said.

"Think it over, guys. A grand each for a couple days' work, and then maybe processing work later. Beats supermarket money."

"We can't take the risk," Matt said.

"Well, I'll tell you what. I'll keep it open as long as I can; I'd prefer you two. I can trust you, and that's important in this game."

"I'm sure it is," Matt said. And he went quiet. Bloody hell, he was tempted at a time when he might need money. He would have to see how things went at work. He had some ideas himself for getting by, but he would have to wait his time to tell BJ about them.

THIRTEEN

MATT LOOKED around the Pier Café; it was quiet in the mornings. He had arranged to meet Kristy there, but she wasn't inside. Then he spotted her sipping a coffee at an outside table. One good thing about working nights was that not many people were around during the day. He and Kristy had it pretty much to themselves, but he knew there would be a scramble for coffee and croissants around 10 a.m. when the workers were on their break. He wasn't into that sort of food, but he did love a hot pie washed down by a cold milkshake. He had to be careful not to suck too hard on his straw, or it caused an ache on the roof of his mouth. The fresh-baked smell of the pies and savouries got his stomach going, so he wandered over to the counter.

"I'll have a steak pie and a strawberry shake," he said to the pretty red-headed assistant.

"That's fine," she said, taking a pie from the warmer, as he spread the appropriate coins on the counter.

"I'll bring the milkshake to your table."

He took his pie outside and sat down in front of Kristy and munched on it. There was not much wind and the air was warm.

"How did the family thing go?" Matt said, looking across the table to where Kristy sat sipping on a latte.

"The usual thing," she replied. "Making polite talk with people you don't really like or know very well."

"One strawberry shake," a young thin waitress said.

"Thanks," said Matt distractedly looking past Kristy and out to sea. Surfers cut up the small regular waves as if they were slicing bread. They were either shift workers like them or on the dole.

"Let's do something." He looked into Kristy's green eyes.

"Yeah. Let's not waste today. Finish your pie and shake and we'll go for a walk."

Matt gulped down the last of his pie and drained his shake as if he were in some sort of eating competition. They walked out onto the sand, where the wind played in their hair and blew Kristy's white muslin dress against her body and showed every curve.

Matt took his flip-flops off to walk in the hot sand and jumped around as if he were doing a war dance. He put them back on fast.

"That'll teach you," Kristy said. The corners of her mouth twitched into a playful smile.

They walked in the loose sand between the children's playground, the Ramp and the high-tide mark. Matt scuffed the soles of his flip flops lightly on the sand as he walked, and they made a high-pitched squeal. They had to dodge around a mother and two little girls playing in the sand, and walked closer to the Ramp car park.

They didn't see him till it was too late. Stretch, the prospect from the Sidewinders, sat on his bike between two cars, having a smoke.

"Not sick of lover boy yet?" he said to Kristy.

They didn't reply and just kept walking.

"Those creeps don't ever give up," Kristy said.

"Just ignore him."

"They freak me out."

Matt watched the surfers out the back as he and Kristy ambled along. The surf was small but they were getting some good rides. The water was clear and dolphins had joined in with them. He could see flashes of silver and blue forms in the waves as they raced the surfers. He always liked it when dolphins were around because they kept the sharks away. The only time he had ever seen a shark was way out the back one day by himself. He got a hell of a shock to see this big fin sticking out of the water, but it was only a basking shark.

"Those dolphins are beautiful," Kristy said.

"Yeah," said Matt. He had a need to put something into words: "Dolphins on a wave surge ...

Gimme that freedom urge."

"Where did that come from?"

"I don't know ... out of the moment."

"If my father knew what a sensitive guy you are, maybe he would change his opinion." She laughed.

"I doubt it. I'll always be a loser in his eyes."

"You've got me."

"Yeah, I'm happy about that."

The beach was pretty empty. A cold onshore wind had sprung up and spray blew off the lips of the waves, but a few surfers stayed on. It scattered some of the loose sand and rubbish around the beach.

"How about walking me to the bus?" Kristy said.

"Sure," Matt said. "I wish I had wheels." He gave her a cheeky kiss on the mouth.

She jumped and stepped back. "That was nice," she said. "But we better go now. I've got to get some text books for uni."

They cut through Brighton Mall. Jack Dawson was in the window of his shop arranging wetsuits and boards when they went past. He waved them in.

"Hello, there, and who's this?" he said, looking at Kristy.

"I'm Kristy, Matt's girlfriend."

"Well, he's a bit of a dark horse. He never mentioned you," Jack said.

Matt grinned shyly. "We haven't been together very long."

"That might explain it. When are you going to start on that board?"

"I'd do it now but I'm walking Kristy to her bus."

"Never mind me," Kristy said. "You go and do it. I'll get myself home."

"If you are sure,' Matt said. "Watch out for Stretch."

"I will. I've got my cellphone."

"OK, I'll see you at work tonight."Jack continued with the window display while talking to Matt. "You go through and set your blank up on the rack, and I'll be there soon to help you make up a template."

When Matt opened the door to the factory the noise of planes and rasps was overwhelming, and the smell of resin was strong in his nostrils. The guys were so intent on their work they didn't notice him. The whole place looked like a blizzard of foam with guys dressed like aliens in masks and goggles.

Jack came in and showed him how to measure the board up. He held out a tape. "Make sure the board is the same on both sides of the stringer, and the rocker fits in evenly. Now cut the template out of this cardboard. Trace around it,and then draw a mark about twenty millimetres proud of it to trim off the blank later."

"Cool," said Matt. "Now you got me going."

He carefully followed Jack's instructions and watched the board shape appear under his hands. What a dream!

"OK, that's probably enough for one day."

"I'm stoked!" Matt's heart raced. He put the blank away and followed Dawson through to his office.

Jack sat at his desk in front of his computer and Matt pulled up a deck chair.

"I can't wait till next time," Matt said.

"Well, that's the sort of passion I like my workers to have."

"Tell me something."

"Sure." Dawson leaned back in his chair.

"Do your workers belong to a union?"

"That's a bit out of the blue."

Matt crossed his legs. "Well, it's just that, where I work, some are and some aren't in a union, and the boss does what he wants."

Dawson put his hands behind his head. "Well, that's an interesting one. Unions have their place for collective groups of workers doing the same or similar jobs. Over the years they've bettered workers' conditions, and it's in the boss's interest to have a happy, motivated team, even though there are still frustrations both sides."

"Like in the supermarket where I work?"

"You could say that. But a divided workforce increases the power of the boss and breaks down the collective power of the workers. Some industries have lost power through loss of workers, like in manufacturing."

"And gone to China?"

"Exactly, and workers here mostly do their own bargaining on individual agreements; their collective muscle is gone."

"Like me." Matt shrugged. "My contract says I'm expected to work as required."

"It can be a problem in unskilled work," Dawson said. "And, if you don't take the job, someone else will. There's very little solidarity."

"It's not fair," Matt said.

"Then it's up to you to change it."

"Nobody's gonna listen to a kid."

"I have," Dawson said. "Stick to your guns. And, to answer your question, my workers are in the union. We are pretty old school around here."

Matt got up. His heart pounded, busting to get at Rick. It all made sense now; all the things Tiny Jones, his teacher, had said came flooding back, too. He had more than enough to throw at Rick tonight. Let him try to rip him off any further. He was ready.

"I'll see you next time," Matt said and made for the door.

Matt made sure he arrived at the supermarket with time to spare. He was lost in thought, stacking potato chips, when Rick sidled up to him. "Just drop what you're doing, Avery."

"I thought you wanted this finished off."

Rick patted his greasy black hair. "You can come back to it later."

The blood pressure rose in Matt's veins. The words just came out. "This wasn't in my contract."

Rick's lips formed into a wry smile. "Contract says you will work as required, Avery. I don't recall anybody standing over you when you signed it."

"I wanted the job."

"And you still want it?" He bared his teeth.

"I want to renegotiate."

"Well, I don't."

"I want to join the union."

Rick's mouth straightened. "That's your choice. Don't you want to think for yourself? Now get to the storeroom, and tidy up or you soon won't have a job."

Matt's fists clenched. He had enough brains to know that if he hit Rick that would be the end to any career; although, he kind of suspected Jack Dawson might understand. But his mother and future employers certainly would not. As for his old man, he didn't care what he thought. He squared up to Rick. "Stuff the contract … stick your stinkin' job." He ripped open a bag of chips and scattered them in the air. "I'm outta here."

Rick grinned. "I was going to fire you anyway. The money you are owed will be in your bank on Thursday. Now pick up your stuff and get out of here."

Matt thumped upstairs and shoved what little stuff he had in a plastic rubbish bag and went to find Kristy.

He was a free man. It was magic, but it was also crap. He had worked hard for Rick and the supermarket and all he had to show for it was a bad reputation. He made a pact with himself then and there to pretend to future employers that he had never ever worked there. That way Rick would not continue to have any power over him.

Kristy was putting out green bananas when Matt tapped her on the shoulder.

She looked around. "What are you up to?" She looked

at the bag over his shoulder. "Has Rick got you putting the rubbish out now?"

"No. We had a big bust-up. I told him he could stick his job. This is my stuff."

Kristy stopped what she was doing. "Well, that was a bit stupid, wasn't it?"

"No! I was sticking to my guns.""But how are you going to live?" She stroked the side of his face.

"I've got an idea that doesn't include shitheads like him."

"Well, I hope it's a good one."

"It is. I'll catch up with you at the beach."

"OK, good luck."

He swung the bag over his other shoulder and hitched in the direction of home. BJ's phone was on voicemail, which meant he had turned it off. His mother was working. He wondered how long he could keep the news from her.

FOURTEEN

MATT LAY in bed sucking on a joint. He had his door on the snib, in case his mother made a surprise visit. He liked this new house. It might be more humble than their other one but it had more character. He watched the sun twinkle through the leadlight window that overlooked the beach through a gap in the dunes. It was like his little upstairs world; he didn't regret for a minute leaving his other life behind. The smoke tasted sweet and stuck to his throat as he inhaled. It was a great morning and he had that ecstatic feeling of nowhere to be and nothing to do. The only problem was a distinct lack of funds. He wouldn't have worried if it was just him but he hated letting his mother down. He lay there allowing all the random thoughts for raising money to seep into his mind — one concerned stealing cellphones from a local lock-up.

Matt could always hear his mother's feet on the stairs before he saw her. It was a good warning. He extinguished the joint in the glass ashtray on the bedside table and slipped out of bed. It smouldered so he opened a window before opening the door to his mother. She would think it was a cigarette, which she didn't approve of either but it was the lesser of the two evils.

His mother looked tired as she walked into the room and sat in Matt's tattered La-Z-Boy chair. She had the beginnings of dark rings under the eyes and she was worn down. This was down to him as well as his father. "I think you need to take things easy for a while. How about throwing a sickie tomorrow?" Matt said.

"I wish I could. Things are not good." She crossed her legs and sighed. Empty beer bottles lay where they had been discarded; there was even an empty Jack Daniel's whiskey bottle on the dresser, the last of his father's. Matt forbid her to tidy up in his room. He liked it how it was. "You have to get your life together and stop the drinking, and I'm scared to think of what other things you might be doing." She picked up the old Coca-Cola bottle he used as a bong. "At least get rid of your empties."

"I'll sort it." He slouched back on the bed and pushed his pillow under his shoulder for support.

"I'm having trouble meeting the bills." Her mouth was hard and straight.

"Things will get better."

"I know you've been let down, by your father and others, but I need you to step up." Her hazel eyes grew big and sad.

"I've got an idea that could make us megabucks." And he grinned as if a light bulb had gone on in his head.

"That's as may be but ..."

There was a knock on the front door, and they could hear BJ shouting out: "Hello, anybody home? It's only me."

"Up here!" Matt yelled in reply. And they could hear the thump, thump, thump of BJ's heavy footfalls on the polished wooden stairs. BJ strode into the bedroom and Matt's mother got up and said, "I'll leave you boys to it."

"Cool, Mrs Avery," BJ said. He sat down in her chair.

Her footsteps disappeared down the stairs, and Matt considered it safe to run his plans past BJ.

"It's like this," Matt said. "I was at the golf course last week. You know how the properties back onto the course?" His breathing came in short bursts and his face lit up.

"Yeah, so what?" He raised his eyebrows. "What's so intriguing about that?"

"I saw old man Johnson from Johnson Electronics in the city unloading cameras and phones into his garage the other day. I'm sure it's not even alarmed. I can soon take care of the lock on the side door. He's probably only got a padlock on it. Bolt cutters will take care of that." Matt grinned wide, showing even white teeth.

"You're mad. This is serious stuff; it's not like robbing your old man."

"We aren't going to get caught; come on, it'll be a hoot." He threw an empty Coke bottle at him from the bedside cabinet.

"If we get caught, it will ruin our lives." BJ threw the bottle back.

"Mine's already blown out like the surf on a bad day."

"Mine's not ... but I can't let you go alone."

"Now you're talking. We'll go tonight after dark." Matt got up from the bed and looked out the window. "The surf's crap. Want a smoke?"

"Sure," BJ said. "If it's good stuff."

"It is. And it's the last of it until I get some more funds."

They smoked and planned what they would need to take with them to pull off a successful heist.

They waited for darkness like kids waiting to set off fireworks. Matt pulled at the shoulder straps on his pack. There was nothing in it, yet the straps were digging into him, so he took it off and adjusted the straps. The Avondale golf course was accessible from the club house end. They didn't want to be seen, so they sneaked through someone's property on Waratah Street, on the west side of the course. The house they were after was on the other side of the links.

They were under cover from the darkness and trees planted between the fairways. Johnson's property had a wooden paling fence along the boundary. It was about two metres high with a gate built into it. Matt found a large crack in a wooden paling and was able to observe the goings on at the Johnson house through the crack. He watched Mrs Johnson in what he thought was the kitchen window. When the window was clear, he climbed over the paling fence and whispered to BJ through the crack: "Keep an eye out."

"I will," BJ said. "Be careful."

Matt made a run for it to the shelter of a trellis of roses that sheltered him from the view of the kitchen windows. He was very nervous that the house security lights might come on, but so far he was all right. The garage was in shadows and he was sure he couldn't be seen from the house. He made his move from the safety of the rose bush, and took his bolt cutters from his backpack and prepared to cut off the padlock. The second he snapped through the lock there was a flashing of lights and a siren sounded as if it were signalling a tsunami or something. He took to his heels and was soon through the gate, but BJ was already across the fairway disappearing into the trees. He didn't look behind him, and knew for certain the whole neighbourhood would be alerted, which could mean cops and dogs.

They went back the way they had come, and Matt ditched his backpack under a rhododendron. He didn't want to be seen walking down the road, which would be an open invitation to the cops. Back at the gap in the fence, where they came in, they saw the flash of red and blue lights go past out on the road. Matt wondered if they were looking for them. At least they were now on the opposite side of the golf course. He hadn't touched anything at the garage, so there wouldn't be any prints, and he didn't think anybody saw him running away. They wouldn't have a description. They were in the clear even if the cops stopped them, he was pretty sure.

They cut around the back of the golf links, hit Wainoni Road near the top end, and walked along brisk and upright. They were about a kilometre from the crime scene and in darkness, except for street lights. BJ nudged him gently as a cop car slid to a halt beside them. Two officers got out and called them over to the car.

"Put your hands on the car," said the one with the moustache. It was those same cops again. He manhandled them into position with their hands and legs shoulder-width apart.

"I know my rights," Matt said as he wriggled out of the constable's grasp.

"You're a suspect; do as I say," said the other officer, Sykes. The skinny one, Wilson, didn't say much and watched them both with a suspicious eye as they leaned against the roof of the Holden prowl car.

"They look clean," said Sykes.

"They may be clean now but I've got my eye on these guys."

'Of course we are clean! What did you expect?" Matt stood upright and loosened his shoulders.

"I've watched you around the beach, and one day I'll bust the lot of you," said Sykes.

"Are you going to arrest us?" BJ said.

"There may not be evidence to arrest you guys, but

that doesn't mean you're not guilty of that break-in down the road," said Sykes.

Both cops then clambered back into their car and drove off.

"I've had enough excitement," BJ said.

"Me too." They walked back to the Hilux, which was parked down a side street, and BJ drove Matt home.

Matt's mum had her nose in a book when he came through the door. She looked up at him. "I left you a chicken snack in the refrigerator." She went back to reading her book.

He sat down on the couch. "I'm not hungry."

"The local paper's here if you want to improve your opportunities." She indicated that it lay beside her. "There are a few jobs advertised better than the supermarket." She put her glasses on her nose and looked over them at him.

"Nah, I'm not interested in another nine-to-five job. If I was, there's much more choice online. I'm going to make some real money." He put his feet up on the coffee table.

"Just like your father." She frowned. "Get your feet down!"

"Nothing like him. That's my point. I'm tired. I think I might go upstairs."

"Good night, then, but you've got to sort yourself out sooner or later."

"Let's make it later." He spun on his heel and made

his way up to his room. How was it you always managed to hurt those you love? It was trite but quite true where he and his mother were concerned. She didn't need to know he had lost his job yet. He would wait till the time was right.

He trudged up the stairs as if his shoes were filled with cement. He turned on the bedroom light, shook his running shoes off and then plonked on the bed. He didn't want a drink or smoke but the *Anthology of Romantic Poetry* caught his eye on the bedside table. He randomly flicked through it looking for some inspiration.

Then he saw a couple of lines of Keats and read them quietly to himself aloud:

"Beauty is truth, truth beauty, — that is all
Ye know on earth, and all ye need to know."

It resounded in his brain like a divine equation. That was the poetic equivalent of $E = mc2$. He certainly knew Kristy was beautiful, and he didn't have to wonder how much truth was in that, but it spurred him on and encouraged him to think people had other values outside the day-to-day struggle and they were usually hip-hop artists, poets, painters or the like. It might be something to base your dreams on, and he grasped a vision that didn't come out of a bottle or the suck end of a bong, even though Coleridge was known to be partial to a few opium dreams. But it seemed to Matt beauty had turned skank and truth was a dirty word in the public vocabulary. How could you know truth and beauty if your currency was ugliness and lies? And it was up to him to get his shit together. How could he live his own life and help his mother when the drugs had him in their grip, the cops were on his tail … and the money was running out?

FIFTEEN

MATT AND BJ sat with their backs to the stone sea wall at North Beach looking out to sea. The onshore wind tousled Matt's mop of brown sun-bleached hair, and the sun warmed his lean upper body. There was a lone surfer out the back, a guy he had seen the Burrows brothers hanging out with. He was surrounded by squawking seagulls diving for sprats. The surf was average to small and the guy had to wait quite a while for a decent wave. It was good to have BJ with him. BJ was lucky he worked for his old man detailing cars and could pretty much work when he wanted to. If he didn't work, the rest of the team would take up the slack — lucky for some.

But Matt didn't have his old man to fall back on. He had to find his own way. In the meantime, he would just enjoy the freedom of being without a job. He could go and register for the dole but it wasn't worth it. They had a stand-down period before you got any money, and it was piss-all anyway. They would find him a job the same as the one he had left with some little Hitler for a boss.

The seagull squawks were joined by the sound of a VW air-cooled motor behind him. When Matt stood up and turned around it was Kobe in his beach buggy. He yelled out from the buggy, "Hi, guys, wanna go for a cruise?"

"Sure," Matt yelled back.

"I'm in," BJ said.

Matt jumped in the front and BJ over the back. It was a nice day for cruising. Matt watched the world whizz past; it was like being on a motorbike except you didn't need a helmet, and it was more comfortable.

They did a few circuits of Brighton township, and then pulled up onto the Ramp car park by the surf club. There weren't many cars around, just a few campervans and people walking dogs. They sat silent, looking out to sea, but Matt studied Kobe's face on the sly. He had the face of an old rock-and-roller, but he was only in his early twenties. His hair was strawberry blond and spiky, and his skin was pockmarked from once-bad acne. He was wiry. He wore a thick gold chain around his neck, tired jeans and a black T-shirt with a marijuana plant emblem on it.

Kobe kept his gaze on the sea. "Thought any more 'bout my offer?"

Matt focused on the waves. There were a few teenage kids with body boards in the inshore break probably bunking off from school. "What offer was that?"

"Don't go silly on me — you know. I've got some weed to harvest and only a short time to do it."

Matt kept his gaze on the kids in the surf. "I'm kinda looking for a job, and …"

"Might be risky," BJ cut in.

"It'll be a piece o' piss." Kobe finally turned to look at them. "Away from the cops."

Matt rubbed his chin as if he had a goatee. "Might be a blast. A grand each, you reckon?"

"Yup, you wanna shake on it?" He held his hand out to Matt.

"I'll trust ya," Matt said.

"Hope it's better than your last idea." BJ smiled at Matt.

"Kobe's face lit up. "What idea was that?"

"Never mind," Matt said. "When do we go?"

"Tomorrow morning."

"OK," Matt said, "you'd better drop us off. We've got to sweet-talk our oldies and get our stuff ready."

"Looks like it's all on," BJ said.

Matt burst through the front door. His heart raced. He yelled out, "Mum, Mum, where are you?"

But then he remembered it was pay day. His mum always did the groceries on pay day, and it was one of her days off from her job as hospital cook. Sunday was the other. She worked all sorts of funny shifts so they weren't often at home together. The lounge had that freshly vacuumed smell it got when the ratty carpet had its fibres stirred up. He looked over to the kitchen at the old stainless steel bench top and the scuffed linoleum floors. They gleamed. His mother had done her clean. She liked to do that bright and early. And it knocked home how little he did round the place. He only cut the lawns — and not until they were long and lank. Then he would have to mow them without the catcher, and they would look like a freshly mowed field of hay.

There was a toot-toot from the drive, the signal for him to come and help her with the bags of groceries. Matt grabbed most of the bags and his mother took the remaining two and followed him into the house. They put them on the bench, where his mother began to unpack them as they talked.

Matt leaned on the counter. "I left my job at Food World. But the good news is I've got a job with Jack Dawson. We'll still have money coming in." He took in a big breath waiting for her reply.

"Well, I can't say I'm disappointed about the grocery boy job, but, really, can't you do better than making surfboards? Where's the money or security in that?"

"You'd be surprised, and, by the way, I'll be away for a couple of days with Jack on a buying trip."

"Well, if you must, dear, but I can't see a future."

"We're going to camp out and get some surfing in, as well. You don't mind if I take these sausages and a few cans of beans?"

"I thought a businessman like him would be staying in a five-star hotel."

"No, he likes to keep his feet on the ground and remember where he came from."

"Very well."

"I'll get my sleeping bag and a couple of blankets from the hall cupboard."

"If you are sure. How are you travelling?"

"BJ's going to pick me up in the morning and drop me off at Jack's. I just have to make sure everything's ready."

"Good, I'll see you off. Wake me if I'm not up."

"OK, Mum, and remember there could be big money in this new job."

"Well, it's good to see you in a happier frame of mind. More money's always a bonus."

"It's all good."

The piercing alarm on Matt's cellphone brought him out of a dead sleep. He was having such a nice dream locked in Kristy's arms. It was two minutes past eight. His head spun with everything they had to do. Cool, his mother didn't suspect anything. He didn't really want her to see him off. He just wanted to disappear and get the job done as quickly as possible and without any drama.

Matt heard the Hilux pull up at the gate. His mother walked out with him. He put the last of his gear in the back of the Hilux, and gave his mother a reluctant hug and jumped into the cab beside BJ. He wound his window down. "I'll see you when I see ya, and don't worry."

BJ tooted and they ripped off into the morning to collect Kobe.

Kobe was waiting on the footpath outside his house with all his gear at his feet. He had a pile of empty synthetic woolsacks to put the weed in.

Matt and BJ sat in the truck while Kobe loaded it. He finished and jumped in behind them.

"Where to?" BJ said.

"Head west, young man: I'll show you as we go."

They drove through the eastern suburbs and then took State Highway 73, the West Coast road. There wasn't much traffic, just the usual farmers in their pick-up trucks with sheep or pigs on the back, and sheep trucks and trailers loaded up for the freezing works. Matt felt sorry for the sheep. Every time one of these big trucks accelerated past, he got a whiff of diesel fumes.

There wasn't much out that way — mainly sheep farms and Paparua Prison. It was flat and arid country until you got near the foothills where it greened up a bit. And there were clusters of native forests in the valleys. This was the direction they were headed but Kobe hadn't said exactly where. The road was flat and straight and Matt could see the Alps; even at this hot time of the year there were little caps of snow on the peaks.

The sides of the road were now cut off from the farmland by huge macrocarpa hedges, which gave shelter from the blustery winds that swept across the plains. They came to a little town called Darfield. This was pretty much the centre of the first quake in September. It sat near the east–west railway line. It had little more than a pub, supermarket, garage and souvenir shop. They filled up the Hilux and got themselves a pie and a Coke for breakfast. Kobe munched on his pie. "It's not far from here," he said. "Keep on going west, and I'll tell you where to turn off."

They came to an old graveyard with freshly broken headstones. The whole area, on the corner of a main road, was surrounded by a rusty wrought iron fence. "Turn right here," Kobe said.

BJ turned, crossed the railway line, and they were now on a bumpy secondary gravel road. Matt could almost taste the dust in his throat between the thuds of the Hilux tyres in the potholes. He took a swig of cold Coke, which soothed his dry throat. "I don't like the road much," he said.

"Keep on going up this road until you come to an old wooden gate," Kobe said.

When they came to the gate, Matt got out, opened it and then shut it behind them. "This is government land," Kobe said. "They never come here. They check it out from time to time by helicopter."

They followed two wheel tracks through the long grass. Soon the tracks ran out and BJ was driving through open paddocks. Kobe pointed them to where some bush grew up the valley.

"Where's the weed?" Matt said.

Kobe pointed. "In a clearing in that bush. We should be able to get the truck up there and camouflage it."

"OK," BJ said.

"It's only ten a.m.," Matt said. "It won't take two days."

"I just wanted to cover all the bases. Don't worry, guys, if it only takes a day you'll still get your full money. The quicker we get out of here the better."

"I'm all for that." BJ drove the Hilux up to the edge of the bush. They cut some broadleaf and tree ferns and draped them over the roof and bonnet of the truck. From a distance it looked like part of the bush. They took their slashers and grabbed the woolsacks as well. It was only a short trek to the marijuana crop that glowed in its distinctive light green and stuck out from the other growth around it.

"Just take a breather before we start," Kobe said. "I want a nosy around."

"Cool," Matt said, "take your time."

"It's OK to start." He threw them each a woolsack. "Fill 'em up."

"You've made a good job of the weeding," BJ shouted in Kobe's direction.

"Someone has to do the hard yards!" he shouted back.

They sliced through the stems of the marijuana as if it were asparagus. Then they chopped them into shorter pieces that would fit in the bags. The plants looked healthy and ready for harvesting. The sweat poured off them and the whole six woolsacks were full in no time.

They dragged the packs to the truck but then they

had a problem. Only two of the sacks would fit in the back. And Kobe would have to position himself around them if he wanted a ride home.

"OK, guys," said Kobe. "We're going to have to go back to Darfield and hire a trailer."

"I've got a better idea," Matt said. "We've got plenty of rope; we'll put two on the roof rack and two inside and come back for the rest tomorrow. Let's hope we will be mistaken for alpaca farmers taking their wool to market. A bit like hiding in open sight."

"I can't believe you didn't think about this before," BJ said.

There was the crack of rifle shots from the other side of the hill. They all looked at each other. "Hunters!" Kobe said. "They could be here soon. Right, let's get the other two on the roof and get out of here." They got four woolsacks aboard the Hilux and jumped in.

Matt hated leaving the two sacks behind, but what could they do if the shooters came over the hill?

They were nearly at the gate to the road when five shots rang out in rapid fire from an automatic rifle and shattered the back window. The further impact had been taken by the two tightly compressed woolsacks, so no one was injured. Matt took a quick look back, and he saw two black figures standing by the woolsacks they had left behind. BJ planted his foot and very soon they were through the gate and on their way to safety. They breathed a sigh of relief, and settled to the steady rumble of the Toyota engine. Out of the awkward silence, Kobe cleared his throat and leaned over the seat. "Bloody hunters ... of all days." His face was glum.

"Hope they don't phone the cops," BJ said.

"They won't do that," Kobe muttered.

There was a lengthy silence. Matt caught BJ's eye and frowned. Something didn't stack up. "What's going on, Kobe?" he said.

"Aw, nothing."

"There bloody is ... spill it!"

"Um ... they weren't hunters. They were Sidewinders."

"What?!" BJ and Matt screamed together.

BJ stopped the Hilux. "You've got to be kiddin' us."

"I figured it was payback time," Kobe said, "for when they plundered my crop last season. Besides, look at the way they've treated your girl."

"You've dropped us right in it." Matt glared at Kobe.

BJ paled. "We're in deep shit."

"Relax," Kobe said, "they don't know who we are. That's why I had to tell you, so you will keep your mouth shut."

Matt wiped his brow. The Sidewinders didn't know who they were yet, but they would find out. He wasn't fooled for a minute. They got a glimpse of the truck even if it was just a rear view. One thing was for sure, there was no going back.

SIXTEEN

"STOP!" KOBE yelled. He pulled at a crinkly blue tarpaulin at his feet. "We better put this over the stuff on the roof. It's too obvious what's in the sacks."

"I did worry about that," Matt said. "We'd be lucky to get through Darfield like this."

"Yeah," BJ said. "We want the cops to think we are alpaca farmers taking wool to town."

"Let's hope," Kobe said. They lashed the cover down over the weed and jumped back in the truck fast.

All the time, Matt worried the bikers might catch up with them, but they didn't seem to have a vehicle anywhere handy. They would have cellphones, though. In case the shooters had phoned for help, they took the road north across the Waimakariri River and back into town a roundabout way.

The Sidewinders would probably come the shortest and most direct route.

They were now motoring steady again. The Hilux had settled into an even hum with the wind buffeting the sacks and rippling through the cover on top. They turned off at Darfield, over the railway line, and, after a while, crossed the river. Windswept paddocks and pine plantations flew past, and soon they were slowing for the city limits.

Going this way they saw very little traffic.

BJ checked his rear-vision mirror. "Motorcycle coming up fast. Shit!"

"Can you see him? Is he wearing patches?" Kobe asked.

"Nah, it's all right. It's a guy on a farm bike," Matt said as the bike overtook them.

They linked up with the northern motorway and headed south, which took them to the city limits. Then they meandered their way through town to Avoca Valley, where Kobe's friend lived in a tired old stucco cottage on an acre of land. It was an area of prime market garden and orchard land. His property nestled into a north-facing hillside, which had been part of a bigger property used as accommodation for workers. It had a long metal drive and at the back of the house was a sort of depot flanked by farm buildings. They off-loaded the weed into the three-bay implement shed.

There was a rusty corrugated iron room at the back that had makeshift racks for drying and a wooden bench along one side. The cops could search Kobe's place as much as they liked, but he kept his stash here.

After they stacked the sacks away in the shed, Kobe went to his inside jacket pocket and reeled off two bundles of five hundred dollars in fifty-dollar notes.

A pungent smell filled Matt's nose. He wasn't sure

whether it was nearer to hay or freshly-mown grass, but maybe that was why it was sometimes called grass.

"I'm sorry, guys," he said. "I had hoped we would be bringing another two woolsacks out. I can't go back now; we all know why."

"That's not good enough," Matt said, as Kobe handed them the notes.

"It's not what we agreed," BJ said. "We took a big risk for you."

Kobe's eyes lit up. "I'll tell you what; I'll pay you in kind." He went inside the house and came back with a sealed plastic bag full of weed. He passed it to Matt, who slid the zip lock and sucked in the distinctive sweet smell.

Kobe snatched the bag. "Give me that money back and I'll give you this three-hundred-gram pack of weed, which has a street value of around three thousand bucks."

"Sounds like a deal," Matt said. "We're already in deep shit." He snatched it back.

But BJ was hesitant. "It's going to take a while to get our money back, and there's a risk of getting busted, not to mention serious action from the Sidewinders."

"Right!" Kobe said. "But that's not going to happen to you. Only deal with people you know, like the stoners from your old school. The Sidewinders know shit … besides, this is not their stuff; it's mine, primo heads. It comes from the flowering female cannabis plant. The most potent part." He laughed. "Just sort of thought I would throw in a bit of product knowledge."

Matt and BJ got in the truck with their bag of weed.

"Just one thing," Kobe said. "Stay away from my customers."

"Nothing like a bit of competition," Matt shouted through the open passenger window.

Kobe ran over to Matt's open window. "Hey, guys, did I tell you? There's a party on at the Burrows brothers on Saturday night."

"We'll keep it in mind," Matt said. "Who knows, I might get some new clients."

BJ turned the truck around and they headed for his parents' holiday shack over the hill from Sumner to Taylors Mistake.

"We'll shove the stuff in the garage," BJ said. "We hardly use the place at the moment."

"Yeah, it's risky keeping the stuff at home." Matt put the bag under the front seat.

The road to Taylors wound up the hill from Sumner amidst upmarket houses with views across Pegasus Bay. The view stretched west over the jagged skyline of Christchurch city to the snow-capped mountains and north arching up the east coast of Pegasus Bay well beyond New Brighton. On a clear day you could see the Kaikoura mountain range. The road descended just as twistedly into the delightful cove nestled between two rocky headlands. Vigorous surf smashed onto the beach of Taylors Mistake, which was backed by a row of sand dunes.

It always brought back good memories to Matt of the times he and BJ used to run around the base of the cliffs, where little shacks had been built into the cliff faces right on the rocky water's edge. Only one remained now. They would play pirates and run around with makeshift cutlasses made from driftwood. BJ's family bach was on the hill overlooking the bay. BJ drove the Hilux down the drive to the garage that was off the main road into Taylors, partly hidden by trees.

They entered the garage, and Matt placed the weed in the back of the bottom drawer of the workshop bench. He shoved plastic bags of nails in front of it. "Should be OK here," he said.

"Yeah, great. That will take a bit of finding." BJ fumbled around in his father's toolbox and found an old padlock and key.

"This will keep anybody out," BJ said. "Not that anyone comes here."

"That's cool." Matt's cellphone ringtone made the sound of a crashing wave.

"Who was that?" BJ said.

"Kristy. She wants to meet us at North Beach. We'll take orders and sell them in three-gram, fifty-dollar bags," Matt said. "We won't carry big amounts around."

"Sounds like a plan." BJ snapped the lock onto the garage door and took the key.

"Keep the key in the glove box," Matt said. "Then we both know where it is."

When they got to North Beach there was no sign of Kristy, only Mullet and Stretch. They sat on their bikes in the car park at the entrance to the beach. BJ pulled in beside them and Matt leaned over to the driver's window. "You guys haven't seen Kristy, have you?" He was terrified they might see the broken back window, and have heard about the raid on their marijuana plot. They just blabbered on. Stretch twisted around on his bike to talk to Matt.

"The little hottie? I saw her a while ago. She's still playing hard to get."

"She's already sorted, so hands off." The blood rose in Matt's body.

"What she needs is a real man." Stretch's lips curled in a sleazy smile. "I bet you haven't even screwed her yet."

Matt raced out of the truck and grabbed Stretch by the collar of his cut-off denim jacket. "What'd you say?"

"I was right, was I?" Stretch grinned, showing yellow teeth.

Matt threw a right hook at Stretch's head, but Mullet was off his bike now and grabbed his arm.

BJ slid out of the truck, and Matt took that as a signal to back off for now, but he bristled inside with sick satisfaction. It was a good feeling to know they had ripped the Sidewinders off and they had no idea.

"She went that way." Stretch pointed to the north. "Walking the hots off, I guess."

Matt wasn't going to answer that. He would save it up for another time if he ever got Stretch alone.

He could take him if he was by himself, no worries. Mullet's cellphone rang and whatever the message was it must have been important because they both jumped on their bikes and roared off at full throttle down Bowhill Road.

Matt and BJ walked north along the beach and they saw a lone silhouette coming towards them. Matt couldn't be sure but it looked like Kristy. They kept walking at a brisk pace. It was her, and when they got close they saw she was sobbing into her handkerchief. Matt put his arm around her. "It was those bloody Sidewinders, wasn't it?"

"Yup," Kristy said. "Filthy pigs!" She blew her nose. "They asked why I only have one boyfriend." She cuddled in tight to Matt's chest.

"The dirty bastards," BJ said.

"That's exactly it, and then they started grabbing at my top and lifting my skirt up. It was mainly Stretch trying to win points, but the other one went along."

"I'll kill them." Matt's face flushed red.

"We should get the police," BJ said.

"No!" Kristy said. "I don't want to give them an excuse to attack me."

"Don't worry," Matt said, "their time will come." And

he smiled to himself, knowing in a way it already had.

A gold SUV pulled up where the bikers had been parked.

"That's Mum," Kristy said. "I texted her to come and get me. I'd better go."

"I'll ring you later." Matt released her from under his arm.

Matt watched Kristy climb safely into her mother's car. He turned to BJ. "Let's go to mine and get us a bacon and egg burger. I'm starving."

They jumped in the Hilux and cruised down Marine Parade with both windows down, which filled the cab with warm air.

They parked two doors down from Matt's place behind a trendy black 911 Porsche.

"We're home!" Matt shouted as he walked through the front door. BJ followed close behind him. His mother was in the kitchen emptying the dishwasher. She turned around, startled. She stood up. "I wasn't expecting you until late tomorrow." Then she saw BJ. "Oh! Hello, BJ."

"Hi, Mrs A," BJ said.

"Sit down and tell me all about your trip, dear," Matt's mother said. Matt and BJ both slouched down on the couch.

"We're starving! There's nothing to tell. Just a boring buying trip … I mostly looked on."

"What would you like to eat?" she said.

"One of your bacon and egg burgers," they said in unison.

His mother's face beamed. "Coming right up." She grabbed some buns and mince patties from the freezer, and then buzzed them separately in the microwave. She shouted over the top of the microwave. "I saw your father in town today. He had that woman with him; she couldn't wait to tell me they had taken on her son, Liam, at work."

"Tell someone who cares," Matt yelled back, even though he knew it would solve all his financial problems at the moment.

"That should be your job," BJ said.

"Except, I don't want it … or anything to do with them."

"That is your birthright," his mother said.

"There's nothing right about it. I'm gonna be a board shaper." Matt's whole body tensed.

His mother threw several rashers of fatty bacon into the pan and they sizzled in the cooking oil. The aromas filled Matt's nostrils immediately, and his stomach juices went into overdrive. There was nothing like biting into one of his mother's choice burgers with bacon, egg and beetroot. McDonald's didn't have a look in. They were amateurs in this game. Their buns weren't even toasted. They were designed for speed, not a teenage appetite.

The thing was, his father could take on Liam if he wanted to, but it wasn't going to make him any keener;

in fact, it had the opposite effect. The more his father hassled him, the more determined he was to give him the finger. He didn't need him; he had a means of getting by for now, thanks to Kobe, and he had plans for the future with Jack Dawson. His father didn't figure anywhere in his schemes. And the Sidewinders could take a hike. For now, he refused to be limited like his father by something as sucky as the law.

SEVENTEEN

MATT TOOK his blank and placed it on the rack. Since his last visit, Jack had sorted him out a shaping bay away from the main activity of the factory where he could take his time and not interfere with any of the other workers who were on deadlines. The place still reeked of fibreglass resin, but it was good. The smell seemed to take him away from everything that had happened over the last few days. This place was like a sanctuary.

Jack came in to see how he was going. He looked pretty trendy with his long grey locks, designer stubble, loose-fitting khaki shorts and flip-flops. He made Matt's father seem like a creature from another world. It was hard to believe they were the same generation. Jack looked closely at the outline Matt had marked out the previous time.

"OK," he said. "I think you are ready to cut." He handed Matt a handsaw from a shelf behind them. "Have you used one of these before?"

"Yup," Matt said, "building stuff around home."

"OK," Jack said, "it's time."

Matt cut the outline leaving a twenty-millimetre margin to surfoam down later. The foam peeled off in sections. It had the look of the scrapings from a fluffy rice cracker. It felt like it too. Matt put the saw back on the shelf, and they both stood back to admire the image.

"That's got the makings of a versatile board," Jack said.

"I hope you are right." Matt beamed.

Jack leaned against a bench. "How did you get on at your other job? Did you play the union card?"

Matt stood looking at his blank. "Yeah, but then I just told him to stick it."

"Not always the best approach. You're going to need a job."

"I've got things sorted working in sales."

"Well, don't get too cynical. Not all employers are bad and not all unions are good."

Matt ran a hand down the edge of his board. It was rough. "I'll try to remember that."

"I'm surprised you are not working for your father." Jack was poised to go but something seemed to hold him back.

"I think I told you. We don't get on." Matt picked up the trimmings from around the rack. "And anyway the vacancy has been filled by his old tart's son."

"Well, if it's any consolation I never got on with my old fella either, and if you had a bit more experience, I'd consider taking you on."

A plump guy with a mop of curly brown hair and a fibreglass-stained apron came in and approached Jack.

"Cool," Matt said." He was amped up to surfoam his blank down to the line. He took the rasp down from the shelf to get started. It looked like a cheese grater. Jack stopped him.

"I'm afraid that's going to be it for the day. I need the bay for a rushed job, and next time you will need to put on all the protective gear. This stuff's toxic, you know."

"Oh, OK," Matt said. "I'll catch you next time."

He packed up and then texted BJ to pick him up. They had other work to do.

BJ was prompt. Matt watched him pull up outside. The first thing he noticed was the back window had been replaced, but there were still a couple of .22 bullet holes in the tailgate.

They were hard to notice. The major evidence was gone. He jumped in the cab.

"Drive around and watch out for customers," Matt said to BJ. They cruised around up the Ramps and down Marine Parade past all the beaches but they didn't spot anyone. So Matt decided they should park the truck and leg it through Brighton Mall and see how many stoners were hanging around. It would be good to sell now and deliver tomorrow.

Things looked quiet in the mall — just the usual midweek shoppers — but then Matt heard guffawing and laughing. The wind was fresh between shops and they cast shadows that chilled his spine. They came around the corner into the sun and he spotted five stoners smoking roll-your-own tobacco. Either it was too public to smoke weed or, he guessed, they could be fresh out.

"Hey, Avery, wassup?" Joss said. She was a lank-haired girl about eighteen with lip and ear piercings. She had a hungry, pallid look.

"Not much. How you guys going?"

"We're fine, Avery," Joss said. "Just shooting the breeze, waiting for our money."

"Yeah, we're getting low on smoke," Ike said. He was a bit older with long black hair, and he wore a Metallica T-shirt and had a scraggy, tawny beard.

The other three joined in together: "Yeah, waiting for pay day."

BJ stood in silence letting Matt do all the talking.

"I'll tell you what, guys, how would you like to buy a three-gram bag of primo weed for fifty bucks?"

"Maybe," Joss said. "We've been getting it from Stretch up to now … and it's been bad shit."

"Yeah," Ike said. "And he wants big bucks for it. He keeps on telling us they gonna harvest some primo stuff real soon."

"We'd be starters, if you can guarantee it's primo," Joss said.

"Yeah, it's heads … OK, see you here same time tomorrow. You want a bag each?"

"For sure," they all said.

"It's cool doing business," Matt said and smiled.

Matt and BJ wandered back to the car. "That was a good little sesh," Matt said.

"Yeah," BJ said. "But they are Sidewinders' customers." Matt stepped up his pace, eager to get back to the truck.

"Tough." Matt set his mouth in a hard line. "I wanna catch up with Kristy. She's not happy with me about work."

"She's been busy getting ready for uni. Plus her olds aren't too keen on her seeing us."

"That's too bad," Matt said. "You go in and get her. They like you more than me."

Tiny beads of sweat formed on his brow.

They cruised over to her side of town to pick her up, and BJ went to her door. The morning had been cooler with a sea mist, but the mist had cleared and the afternoon was going to be a scorcher. He hoped Kristy would be able to come. He watched BJ and Kristy come out of her house. She looked real hot in pink shorts and a lemon polo shirt. BJ looked rumpled and creased in his Hawaiian shirt and baggy shorts, as if he had just climbed out of bed. She was as bright as the summer's day, and the sun caught the gold highlights in her hair. She was a real vision.

They clambered into the truck. Kristy's sweet perfume overwhelmed Matt, and it was as if he had never been away from her. "How is the job search?" Kristy said to Matt from the back seat.

"It's fine," Matt said. "I've got a job in sales."

"What sort of sales?"

"I'm selling surfboards for Jack Dawson … till he can take me on as a full-time shaper."

"How's that work?"

"I'm sort of freelance. I sell to surfers around the beaches. The money's good and the hours are flexible."

"Oh well, I suppose it's a job of sorts with future prospects."

"Better than my old one — anyway, let's not be boring." They passed a break in the dunes and Matt caught a glimpse of the glittering sea. "The surf looks good."

Kristy reached over the front and put her hand on Matt's shoulder. "Yes, it does," she said.

The sun sparkled off the lips of the waves like liquid diamonds. Matt could not remember when the waves and weather had been so perfect. At North Beach, anyway, it was either crap weather and good waves or good waves and crap weather. It seemed to happen that way. But today was different.

They pulled up at the beach and changed into their surf gear. This is what Matt strived for. He had Kristy by his side and soon they were paddling out into the face of glassy waves that came up to his chest. Not huge, but real quality. The sun was hot on his face. There was already a group of surfers out there making the most of the conditions, a few local grommets and the more experienced. Gulls soared overhead on the thermals. Ben Burrows was amongst the surfers and so was Jake Edwards, BJ's arch enemy. They just sat astride their boards rising and falling with the rhythms of the sea, waiting patiently. But Ben seemed keen to speak to them.

"Hey, guys," he said. "Have you heard?"

"Heard what?" Matt said. He swung his board around with a twist of his hips to face Ben Burrows.

Burrows had their full attention. They all had curious looks on their faces.

"It's unreal! I mean who would be stupid enough?" Burrows said.

"For what?" Matt said.

"To rip off the Sidewinders' cash crop of dope."

"It sounds like maybe a rival gang or something," BJ said. He turned pale. They were all straddling their boards, moving with the sea, and they had missed many good rides to listen to Burrows.

"Whoever it was," Burrows said, "I pity them. I have never seen Snake so psyched up. He reckons he will get them, whoever they are, and crucify them."

"Well, I guess they have to catch them first," Matt said. He watched as the sets got bigger, but he still reckoned Kristy would be able to ride them.

"Yeah," Burrows said. "Well, they know they were in an older model four-wheel-drive, probably a Nissan or Toyota, a red one. But they only saw the back of it from a distance."

"Oh well … I came here to surf," Matt said." Let's do some serious damage to these waves."

Matt had his eye on a nice little wave rising out the back. He turned around ready to paddle for it. Kristy followed. The others were still lost in their conversation, and BJ just straddled his board with a grim look on his face. If he wasn't careful he was going to get taken unawares by one of those waves.

A wave was on them now. Matt and Kristy paddled for all they were worth. Matt felt the momentum of the wave beneath him as it picked up his board. And he looked over his shoulder to his left to see Kristy had caught it too. They both swooped down into the belly of the wave and it split at the peak. He went left; Kristy went right. They rode the translucent unbroken water past the inshore break until the wave died a natural death, and they fell into the water, which was up to Kristy's boobs. They just stood there with white water frothing around them like effervescent suds. It was an opportunity to be alone.

"That was a smooth ride," Kristy said.

"I'm impressed," Matt said. "You must have had a good teacher."

Kristy mock punched him on the shoulder. "Show-off!"

Matt looked out the back to see what the waves were doing and saw Jake Edwards push BJ off his wave. BJ would have to wear it. It was one of the rare times

Edwards had the surfer's code on his side, and he made the most of it. Matt worried about BJ. He would have to stay focused if they were going to keep the Sidewinders guessing.

Matt watched the smaller waves around them break and spread their bubbly white patterns into the clear green water. They splashed cold against his chest.

"Look at that," Matt said. He pointed to a school of minnows darting all around them.

"Yes, it's wonderful," Kristy said.

"It's like the birth of life."

"There is a theory ..."

"Never mind the theories." Matt put his arm around her shoulder. "You OK now 'bout the Sidewinders?"

"I'll never be OK about those creeps." Her mouth set hard. "The best I can do is stay out of their way."

"If any of them touch you again," his whole body flexed," I'll kill them."

"No!" Her eyes blazed. "You stay away from them too."

But Matt didn't answer. He turned his gaze seaward. "There's a good set forming. Last one out the back's a hairy grommet."

"You're on," Kristy said. But as he paddled out, reality hit him like a rogue wave. Staying away from the Sidewinders was easier said than done. Not only had he stolen from them, but he was about to start a little sideline selling weed on their patch.

EIGHTEEN

MATT WAS as good as his word, and so were the stoners. He and BJ had prepared the bags of weed using his mother's cooking scales, and they were ready to supply. It was Saturday. The day was sunny but marred by the cold easterly that gave him goose bumps up his bare arms. He shivered in the shade of the shops. BJ had the hood of his hoodie up, and it made him look as if he was up to no good, so Matt pulled it down. But now BJ just looked plain nervous. There weren't many shoppers around.

Only Joss and Ike had showed. They both looked skinny and were dressed in black. They were going to do the deal for the others. That was fine by Matt as long as they had the money. Ike and Joss sat on a bench seat in the sun. They had cornered what heat there was. The goose bumps on Matt's arms were replaced by a nice warm glow.

"You got the shit?" Ike said to Matt. "We sure have … if you've got the money." Matt patted his jeans pocket.

BJ's face paled, and his mouth twitched at the corners. "We can't do the deal here; too open."

"Where do you reckon?" Joss said.

"In the dunes above the south Ramp," Matt said. "You can see who is around from there."

"OK," Joss and Ike said. "Let's do a deal."

They decided to cut along the beach. When they got to the pier there was nobody under or around it. But the shadow it cast made Matt shiver. There were a few surfers nearby in the water. It was nothing like the original wooden closely piled pier his father had shown him in photos.

They moved south along the beach past the library towards the Ramp. They walked in silence. The loose sand found its way between Matt's thonged toes, so he kicked his flip-flops off and put them in his hoodie pocket.

They were soon nestled down in the top of the dunes overlooking the Ramp, watching out for trouble.

"Right," Matt said, "to show goodwill and to let you know what good shit it is I'm gonna let you have a few tokes on the house."

"Stretch never did that," Joss said. "It was always cash up front."

"Well, you're not dealing with the Sidewinders now," Matt said.

Matt took a joint already prepared out of his T-shirt pocket and a lighter out of his jeans pocket. He lit it up and took a long drag while they walked. It mellowed him out straight away. He passed it to BJ and hoped it might calm his nerves.

BJ passed it to Joss. She sucked it in long and hard.

"You were spot on, Avery. This is premium stuff." And she passed it to Ike. Ike took two drags in close succession. "You're not wrong, guys," Ike said. "Put me down for a grand's worth. This sure kicks ass. I'll pick it up same time, same place next week."

"Sure thing! That's what I like to hear," Matt said.

"You let me have mine for free and I'll get buyers for you," Joss said.

"You're on. This is easier than I thought. The stuff sells itself."

Ike rubbed his hands. "What did William Burroughs, the beat poet, say? 'The drug addict is the perfect consumer.'"

"Cool," Matt said to Joss. "You've got a deal." Matt looked around furtively and then opened the McDonald's bag he had in his hand and showed them five bags of marijuana. "That will be two hundred big ones."

Joss dug the money out from between her smallish breasts and handed them to Matt. "That's minus my fifty." With the business concluded they finished off the joint, and Matt was buzzing from the drug high and from making such a big sale and so easy. He could see the attraction in selling drugs and why people took such big risks. The stakes were high but so was the payoff. They all went their separate ways.

Matt and BJ sauntered down to the Ramp car park. Ben Burrows was standing between two cars in his wetsuit when they saw him.

"Not a bad little wave out there today," Matt said.

"Yeah, you guys should be out there. They aren't big, but they are powerful … you'd have to be quick. It won't be long before that chilly onshore gets up and blows them out."

Their conversation was interrupted by a collective rumble as powerful motorbikes made a circle of the Ramp. It was the Sidewinders. Snake pulled up just behind Ben Burrows.

Snake's eyes were fierce and his mouth was hard under his scruffy greying whiskers. "Hey, Burrows, have you seen that little rat Kobe around the beach? As the cops like to say: we want him to help us with our enquiries."

"No, haven't seen him for a week or so."

Snake turned his head to Matt and BJ. "What about you two snot gobblers?"

"Same," Matt said.

"We will find him, don't worry about that." With that he revved up his bike and roared out of the car park, making the angriest statement he could. Several other bikers rumbled after him.

Matt's ears throbbed and his stomach quivered with the sound left behind. There was no doubt about it; all together the Sidewinders were a scary force to mess with. He looked out to sea. Burrows was right; the waves were too good to miss. But how long were they going to last? In the back of his mind he had a nagging worry. The

Sidewinders were somehow on to Kobe, which meant they could soon be on to them. But for the moment it seemed like Kobe had gone to ground like a cornered rodent. If he had any sense he would be out of town. Matt didn't want to go anywhere near him, even if he had known where he was. It would only draw attention to them. It was every guy for himself. But his worst fear was for Kristy, if anything happened to him.

"Hey, Avery," Burrows said. "You and your mate still up for the party tonight?"

"Yup, you still on, BJ?"

"You know me, Avery; we're like Siamese twins." His brown eyes were cast down.

"And bring the girl," Burrows said. "It's a good chance for you to show her off."

"I don't think it's her sort of thing." Matt flushed red.

"Go on, get a bit of grog into her. Who knows, you might even get lucky." Burrows smiled.

Matt got even redder in the face. "I can't get wasted if she's there."

"I'll keep an eye on her," BJ said.

"No, I'll look after her!" Matt said.

"I take it you guys will be there then," Burrows said. "I'm going for a wave."

"OK, see you tonight," they both said. Matt watched Burrows kick through the soft sand until he reached the hard wet shoreline, where he bent down and snapped on his leg tie. Small tongues of water lapped around him. He trudged into the deeper water, and swooped onto his board in one fluid movement and paddled for the bigger sets out the back. That was Matt's cue to ring Kristy and see how she was fixed for that night. He had talked to her about it before, so she should be up for it.

Her father answered her cellphone. "Kristy's phone. Who is this please ...? Oh, Matthew ... I'll tell her you called."

"Shit! That was her old man," Matt said. "I bet he won't tell her."

"No," BJ said, "he will. He's a funny old bugger ... old school. His word is his bond."

"Hope you're right."

"Yeah, so long as she doesn't say she's going to a party."

"I think she will be clued up to that."

BJ was right. They were halfway back to Matt's when Kristy rang. "Are you still on for the party tonight?" Matt said.

"Of course. Pick me up round the corner from our place at eight p.m."

"Cool."

"I've said I'm going to a girlfriend's."

"Yee-ha!" Matt said.

The party was already under way, and there was the tantalising smell of steak and onions wafting from a barbecue just outside the main entrance. The smells taunted Matt's taste buds and had his mouth watering in anticipation. It was an old-style villa with high gables, and verandas that ran around the north and east sides.

It had once been a glorious homestead with acreage, off Marshland Road, but had since been subdivided into a very basic suburban section that was pretty much all taken up by the house, garage and a sleep-out. It was lucky the Burrows brothers had good neighbours, because the evening looked like being a good one. Matt, BJ and Kristy stood by the barbecue. The boys took a beer can out of a forty-four-gallon drum of ice. Kristy found a can of Bourbon and Cola. They slugged them back, daintily in Kristy's case.

Music blared from inside the house — 'Brown Sugar', vintage Rolling Stones. The Burrows brothers were fans of old school rock and blues. In fact, their taste in music was more like the stuff his father used to listen to. It brought back the memories of their house parties when he was a kid when his father was a freedom-loving surfer, the days before he turned into a money-grubbing fanatic. Those were good days, and Matt wondered why things had to go the way they had. Life before Trish; and it occurred to him sex probably had a bit to do with it too.

A steady flow of guys in jeans and T-shirts and girls in shorts and see-through muslin tops filed past towards the music as if under the spell of a Pied Piper. Jake Edwards, BJ's old enemy, was with them. Their skin and hair glowed from too many hours at the mercy of the elements. They had that weathered look that defined them as surfers or, one way or another, children of the sea.

They left Ben Burrows to watch over the barbecue and greet his guests and went inside the house with drinks in their hands to see what the attraction was. They shuffled down the hallway that featured an ornate plaster arch flanked with pillars and capitals, dodged in and out of party-goers, and then turned into the lounge that had a ceiling of pressed tin roses. There were still cracks in the interior walls that were waiting to be fixed by EQC.

That was pretty much all Matt could see. That and smoke rising above their heads and the sweet smell of weed in his nostrils. The Stones had burst into 'Jumpin' Jack Flash' and the revellers in the room were in a dance frenzy. Condensation ran down the cream walls in tiny rivulets. BJ tapped Matt on his shoulder. "Just going to the toilet." He held his can above his head as he weaved through the crowd.

"Me too," Kristy said. She went to the toilet down the hallway next to the bathroom, and BJ chose the one outside by the laundry.

Matt gave them a moment and then followed BJ outside for a quiet smoke. He was just in time to see Jake Edwards grab BJ by the shirt collar. Edwards swaggered from side to side as if he was drunk already. BJ was still pretty sober. Just as Matt was going to jump in, BJ broke Jake's grip, stepped back and then forward with a combination punch to his head, left then right, which sent Edwards to the ground moaning. A girl with long blonde hair and bright-red lipstick helped him inside.

"I'm impressed," Matt said to BJ. "I doubt you will have trouble with him again."

"If I do," BJ said, "I can handle it."

Kristy came out to find them. "Come back inside," she said to Matt. "I keep getting hit on when I'm by myself."

"You take her in," Matt said to BJ. "I'll just finish off my smoke." As he took the last puff on his cigarette he saw a shadowy figure against the curtain in the sleep-out. There was something about the silhouette backlit by the naked light bulb that seemed familiar. Then he got a clear view through a gap in the curtain. He would know that pockmarked face anywhere. It was Kobe.

That was a real surprise. How long could Kobe keep out of the clutches of the Sidewinders? If they did get hold of him, they would torture him till he spilled his guts about them.

NINETEEN

MATT KEPT focused on the shadow in the sleep-out. The cool night made him shiver as he stood on the porch outside. He couldn't believe his eyes. Then the light went out. He walked over and tried the door but it was locked, and he didn't want to knock or make a noise in case it drew unwanted attention. Damn! What the hell was going on here? He'd have to find Ben over at the barbecue and ask some tough questions. But when he got there Burrows was talking to Stretch.

The last of the sausages sizzled on the hotplate and the aromas were irresistible to Matt's nose. He grabbed one, gave it a squirt of tomato sauce, and rolled it in a slice of white bread. Burrows turned the gas off and placed the rest of the sausages on a paper plate. Matt didn't think Ben Burrows would invite any of the Sidewinders, unless he intended to hand Kobe over. What was going on? When Stretch saw Matt, he sneered in his face. "A bit out of your league, aren't you, sunshine?"

"I could say the same about you," Matt said between bites.

"I'm here for the skirt. I'm going inside to mingle." He caught Matt's eye to make sure the emphasis on the word mingle didn't escape him.

Matt was pulled in two directions. He felt the need to go in and watch out for Kristy but at the same time he had a few urgent questions for Ben. He had a quick look around to see who might be within earshot. There was nobody close. But not to risk it, he spoke in hushed tones. "I saw Kobe in the sleep-out through the curtains."

"You did, did you?" Burrows looked around. "I guess you are wondering. It's complicated."

"Try me," Matt said.

Burrows pulled him over to the garage away from several people who were grabbing a beer out of the drum. "We're helping him out."

"Why?" Matt said.

Burrows whispered. "Years ago I used to surf with Snake, and he was a good guy."

"That's why you're friends?"

"We're not really friends. It's just I've known him a long time. But since he's been with the Sidewinders he's had a real pack mentality."

"Whaddya mean?"

"Well, put it this way. When Kobe stole their weed it was only payback for when they raided a crop grown by him and some of his friends last season."

"I see."

"We didn't invite any Sidewinders, by the way; Stretch just gate-crashed. It's going to be too risky to keep Kobe here. We'll move him to some friends up north tomorrow. I don't have to tell you to keep your mouth shut."

"You can depend on me."

"I thought I could. Now let's go in and keep an eye on your friend Stretch and see what mayhem he's created."

Inside, the dancing had stopped. The party-goers had moved into a more subdued state brought on by the marijuana; the sweet smell still hung in the rooms. The crowds had thinned in the lounge and hallway, and the bedroom doors, which had been open before, were now shut.

Some of the revellers had drifted into some more private activity that Matt could only guess at. But he had a pretty good idea that whatever it was, it did not make for good spectator sport. Those that remained were either making out in full view or involved in what appeared to be meaningful animated discussion. The couches were all occupied. Kristy and BJ shared a big rolled armchair. BJ sat in the chair, and Kristy balanced on the arm. Stretch was slouched on the couch with the mystery woman who had rescued Jake Edwards after his beating. Her hair was strewn in all directions, and her miniskirt had ridden up showing a triangle of crimson knickers. Stretch had one arm around her shoulders, and his other hand clamped on her inner thigh. He yelled out to Kristy, "Eat your heart out, dollface!"

Kristy didn't look over or reply.

Ben Burrows walked over to where Stretch and the

girl sat. The girl giggled when he approached.

He looked them in the face and laughed. "Don't you think it's time you got a room?"

"The rooms are all full," Stretch said. The girl wiggled in her seat and pulled her skirt down, and Stretch released his hand from her thigh.

"You should get a motel," Ben said.

"We don't need it all night."

"What do you think I am," the girl said, "some sort of hooker?"

He didn't answer.

"What about the sleep-out?" Stretch said.

"Gazza's in there sleeping off the booze."

"That won't be a problem; I'll boot him out on his ear."

Burrows was gobsmacked for a moment. "Have my room; it's been occupied long enough."

"Cruisy," Stretch said. "Let's go, sweetheart."

The party had become like a broken wave: all the swell and power had gone out of it and it just collapsed on itself. People slunk off and disappeared into the night, shivering in the cooler air. Matt, BJ and Kristy followed them, after they had thanked Ben Burrows for the party. Matt wouldn't give Kristy's parents any cause for worry; he'd have her home by twelve. After all, she was supposed to be at a girlfriend's place.

On the way through Brighton, Matt saw Joss and Ike

with a group of Goths. They were sprawled on a park bench along the waterfront, smoking and guzzling from bottles. He was reminded he needed the stuff ready for them next Saturday. Such easy money!

They cruised over to the other side of town and stopped near Kristy's house. Matt and Kristy jumped out. Matt pulled her close and nuzzled affectionately into her neck. He was suddenly very aware of the warm fullness of her body. As she breathed softly and drew herself against him, he saw the red knickers of the girl at the party in his mind's eye. He kissed Kristy hard, and wondered about her lower regions. He had an urge to go further, but flagged it for a more appropriate time. He released her from his embrace.

"That was lovely. I had an interesting night," she said.

"Sorry I didn't get to spend much time with you."

"Maybe next time." She looked deep into his eyes. "I better go."

"Good night," he said.

She turned and hurried off. "Sweet dreams!" he yelled after her.

They couldn't be seen from her parents' house, but Matt watched her all the way home to make sure she arrived safely. He got back in the truck, and BJ dropped him at home.

Matt's mother was in bed when he got home. The house was in darkness, so he didn't wake her. He was asleep as soon as his head hit the pillow. The next thing he knew the sun seeped through the gaps in the curtains and shone into his tired, sticky eyes. His head spun with everything that had happened. This was the first time in a while that he had been able to stop and just think about things. Kristy filled his thoughts, and he still had a stirring in his chest and loins. It was a very cool, warm feeling.

There was a light tap on his door and his mother came in with a coffee and some toast, which she placed on his bedside table. She wore an apron and a floral print dress. "I didn't hear you come in last night," she said.

Matt propped himself up on his elbow. "It was after midnight."

He picked up his coffee and slurped it.

"Guess what?" his mother said.

"What?"

"Liam's gone walkabout. So I guess your father will be putting pressure on you to work for them again."

"He should have got the message by now. I'm happy working for Jack."

She drew the blinds and looked out the window at the brilliant day. "You're so stubborn. Where's your vision for the future?"

"I made a thousand bucks in commission this week."

She turned back around to face him. "Good, because I'm relying on it for the rent."

"Don't worry, I'm not like the old man. I'll see you right, Mum."

"I know you will, dear," she said and walked out of the room.

Matt lay back in his bed and gnawed on a piece of toast spread with raspberry jam. He was fine for money now, and perhaps for another few weeks, but what would he do when the weed ran out? And what if Kobe didn't make his escape from the Burrows place? Would he snitch? The question still haunted him. Stretch was too pussy-struck to be suspicious. He went for the 'Gazza in the sleep-out story' like the gullible prospect he was. Prospects only existed to be fall guys for the higher-up patched members. You had to be an idiot to be that.

Matt was thinking about getting up when he heard a ruckus at the front door. It was his father's voice. "Where is he? I want to talk to him now. I bet you've been whispering your poison in his ears."

"He's in his room, but I don't think you should go in," Matt heard his mother say.

The door to Matt's room flung open and his father filled the frame. He was dressed in a reefer jacket and maroon slacks. He eyeballed Matt. "I wouldn't normally bother, but it's too good an opportunity to miss."

Matt sat bolt upright in bed, bare-chested. He didn't want to get up because he was in his underwear. "I'm not interested."

His father moved closer and perched on the end of the bed. "There will never be a better time. Trish is all for it now Liam's left."

"I heard about Liam."

"Yes, but Trish was so upset with him, she even suggested you for the job. Can you believe that?"

"Nothing's changed. You're still a cheat and so is your girlfriend."

His father cast his eyes down and his mouth tightened. "I'm sorry you still feel that way."

"Yeah … well, I already told you I'm gonna be a surfboard shaper."

"That's a pathetic waste."

"Well, what would I be if I came to work for you?"

He ignored the question. "We can work things out. You can still stay here and look after your mother. You'll have a lot more money."

"Well, money isn't everything."

"Try doing without it is my answer to that." And the ends of his lips turned up into the smuggest smile Matt had seen since supermarket Rick. "I think you may have already had some experience of that."

The blood ran from Matt's pounding chest to his head in a flat second. He flung himself out of bed in his undies and waved his arms around. "Get out," he said. "Get out of our house."

His mother heard the racket and came running. "I was worried with all the shouting. I thought you had come to blows."

"No danger of that," his father said. "But I hope one day that he comes to his senses."

"Go, go on, get out," Matt said. "And don't come back." His father stomped out, and the pressure in Matt's veins dropped.

Matt's mother put her hand on his shoulder. "Come and sit down, dear, but first put your dressing gown on."

Matt went and put his gown on. His father's money might solve most of their problems but he refused to sell out. But then, he asked himself, what was selling drugs? Wasn't that more like buying into trouble?

TWENTY

MATT'S PHONE beeped, and he scanned the text. "Shit!" It was from BJ. Kobe had been found battered early that morning at North Beach. It was on the news, but he hadn't heard it. His head still spun from the row with his father, and now this.

The beach was unusually deserted when Matt arrived, especially for a nice hot afternoon with good waves. There was a light breeze off the sea. The sun was hot on his whole upper body as he leaned against the Hilux and looked out to sea. BJ was out in the surf by himself.

Matt got his gear from the truck and paddled out to join him. It was obvious to him that BJ's mind wasn't on surfing when he paddled up to him. He was pale, and his forehead was wrinkled. He was mindlessly rising and falling with the motion of the sea and ignored the good waves.

They both straddled their boards and faced out to sea.

BJ broke straight in. "That will be us next. Kobe probably spilled his guts about us."

Matt smiled. "Don't worry … if they knew anything, they would be on to us by now. It's the weed they want.

I doubt Kobe would tell them about us. He was in for a hiding anyway."

"Well, Avery," BJ took in a deep breath, "I hope you are right."

"What I want to know," Matt spun his board around to face the shore, "is how they found him."

"Could have been those Burrows brothers," BJ said. "I don't trust them."

"Don't stress. I'll find out." Matt scanned the shoreline and saw Kristy arrive and go to sit in the dunes watching them. He waved at her. "Kristy's here. Let's go in." He turned to BJ. "Your mind's not on the surf anyway — not a mention about Kobe, though."

"OK. Why worry her too?"

"Exactly," Matt said.

They headed up to where Kristy sat. Matt unzipped his wetsuit and pulled it down to his waist and let it hang. He lay back in the sand and drank in the sun's rays, letting the sun dry him out. Kristy lay beside him and BJ sat cross-legged in his wettie further over.

"I don't know about anybody else, but I'm starving," Matt said.

"I could murder some fish and chips," BJ said.

"Yeah, me too." Kristy looked at her watch. "We never have them at home, and it is tea time."

"OK, that's cool," Matt said. "C'mon, BJ, let's go over to the truck and get our clothes." Kristy tagged along.

Matt and BJ got dressed, and they all hit the fish and chip shop.

The TV was blasting out a hip-hop song from a group Matt did not recognise, but he quite liked the beat. There was a small queue, so he stood in line to order while the other two took a bench seat along one wall and watched the TV on the wall opposite. The song was interrupted by a news flash. The signature news tune played to a montage of beach shots of Kobe's beaten body in some sand dunes and ambulances and police vehicles milling around. Matt recognised the area as being near the North Beach Surf Club.

The reporter stood at the crime scene with her mousy hair blowing in her face. "An early-morning jogger stumbled on a badly beaten young man left for dead at the high-water mark at North Beach." The camera showed the man being carried to a waiting ambulance on a stretcher. "The victim has been identified as Kobe Jacobs, an unemployed builder's labourer. The police suspect the attack is gang-related, but have no firm leads at this stage."

Matt looked over to where BJ and Kristy sat. They both raised their eyebrows at him.

The shop assistant placed the three parcels on the counter and Matt paid for them. Kristy and BJ took their parcels. They all walked back to the sand dunes eating their chips out of a hole they had made in their paper wrappers.

Kristy let go with a barrage of questions. "That guy on TV — isn't he the guy you surf with sometimes? You know, the red-headed guy with the beach buggy. What do you suppose happened?" She munched on her chips, but her face was one big question mark. "They said gang-related. That's scary."

"There's no telling what happened," Matt said, "but we all knew Kobe was into some pretty dodgy stuff."

"Yeah, he probably upset somebody. It doesn't pay to do that, does it, Matt?" BJ narrowed his eyes at Matt.

"No, it does not." Matt smiled at Kristy. "Don't worry, I'm sure he will be OK."

"Well, I worry about you knowing those sorts of people."

"Don't. It's fine."

BJ frowned. "Yup, it sure is."

They made their way back to the dunes, but on the way Matt grabbed an old rug from the back seat of the Hilux. He spread it on the sand amongst the marram grass, high in the dunes with views over the sea. They sat down. There was no breeze on his face. He looked at the waves and saw that the onshore breeze had dropped. The tide was fully out and the waves were glassy and hollow, about shoulder height, and would be even better and bigger on an incoming tide. He scanned the sky. It was pale blue with wisps of white cloud.

He thought he might catch up with Jack Dawson tomorrow and do some more work on his board, but he would still make sure to squeeze a surf in. Matt looked over to where BJ sat. He had his head down and was still picking away at the last of his chips. He had become more withdrawn after the news flash. Maybe he feared the Sidewinders were closing in on them. Matt had known BJ long enough to know that when he went quiet he was petrified. Matt hoped Kristy didn't notice his reaction to the TV news.

BJ looked up at Matt and Kristy. "I'm sorry, you guys, I think I'm going to have to go. Those chips have given me a crook guts."

"That's not cool," Matt said.

"Poor BJ," Kristy said. "You'd better go."

"Yeah, go and get better," Matt added.

The sun was sinking now, and the air had started to chill. They waved BJ off and cuddled into the blanket.

"I nearly forgot," Kristy said, and dug a bottle of wine and two plastic mugs out of her beach bag.

Matt opened the screw-top bottle and poured them both a large portion. Kristy held her mug high: "To us."

Matt held his up and brushed it against her mug. "Us." And then he felt an urge deep within stir in his chest, and he said in an even voice:

"There is a pleasure in the pathless woods,

There is a rapture on the lonely shore, There is society where none intrudes,

By the deep sea, and music in its roar:"

"Wow," said Kristy, "Byron … 'mad, bad, and

dangerous to know'. With the wine, a double whammy."

They skulled their glasses, and then got down to some serious making out beneath the blanket.

It was eight-thirty a.m. Monday morning had come round quick with all the drama of the weekend. Jack Dawson called Matt into his office when he saw him come through the front door. Dawson looked cool as ever in his khaki shorts, plaid shirt and flip-flops. Matt pulled up a Cape Cod chair opposite him.

"I had a look at your blank," Dawson said. "It's all ready to go."

"Cool," Matt said.

"But first," Dawson stroked the stubble on his chin, 'I hear there was a bit of drama in your neighbourhood over the weekend."

"Yeah, a friend of mine was beaten up. The cops think it was gang-related."

"I know it was, and, if I were you, I would learn to pick my friends more carefully. Kobe Jacobs' reputation goes before him. He's a well-known drug dealer in these parts."

"Well, I sort of knew that, but he's a good guy."

"Well, you should know by now that good guys and drug dealers don't belong in the same sentence."

"He's just a surfing mate, really, nothing more."

"Well, I'm just telling you what I know."

"Cool."

"Just stay clear unless you want some of the same treatment from the Sidewinders."

"That who you think did it?"

"Yes, but I have no proof. So if I were you I would stay mighty clear of both parties."

"Thanks." Matt blushed.

"You can thank me by having nothing to do with any of them."

"OK, now can I go and finish my board?"

"For sure."

Matt set his blank up on the rack. He surfoamed and then sanded the edges till they were smooth to his touch. There were fluorescent lights set at about waist height to show any humps or hollows he couldn't feel.

He fine-tuned the edges using a sanding block, sanding and more sanding. Both edges had to be the same. It took him quite a while to achieve that.

Jack came in and admired the edges. "The next stages can be tricky. I'll get Barry to come in and supervise you. Normally I couldn't spare him, but he's between glassing jobs."

"Cool, I might as well finish ... I'm dirty now."

"I'll be in the office if you need me."

A minute later Barry came in. He had bushy brown hair and wore resin-smeared overalls. "Ready to go?" he said.

"Yup." Matt put his mask, and goggles on.

Barry measured the thickness of the blank with

calipers so they would know how much foam to mow. "Just make light passes with the plane till you get the feel of it." Barry put his safety gear on.

"OK," Matt slipped his earmuffs on.

Soon the bay looked to Matt like one of those snow globes with flecks of foam everywhere — down his shirt and throwaway jumpsuit, in his hair and even in his shoes

Forming the board went well with Barry's assistance. And after hours of planing, rasping and sanding, the well-worked blank was ready for paint, finning and glass.

Jack popped his head in the door, then came in and inspected it. He ran his hands and eyes all over the rails. "Nice ... bloody natural," he said in Matt's direction. "That's one hot little board. Clean up and call it a day."

Matt's chest glowed warm. It was a rare feeling getting a bit of praise. "Barry helped a lot," he said. He cleaned up the bay and then ducked into a local café to get a sandwich. It was mid-afternoon. He approached the counter and then heard voices from a booth deep in the shop. "Hey, over here." It was Joss and Ike. Matt got his beef sandwich, went over and sat down with them. The place had a nice homely smell of baking and freshly brewed coffee. The lighting was quite dim in the back where they sat, lit by half-moon-shaped wall lights. Joss and Ike looked like a couple of ghouls with their black hair and pale faces.

"I suppose you've heard about Kobe," Joss said.

"Yeah," said Matt. "I'm still wondering how it happened."

"Well, apparently," Joss said, "Stretch had stayed over at the Burrows' place and he went out the back for a slash and saw Kobe doing the same thing. He tipped off Snake and the rest is history."

"The Burrows should have kicked Stretch out as soon as he arrived," Matt said.

"Yeah, I reckon," Ike said. "You oughta be careful. News has got around to him that some new kid is selling on their patch. And he doesn't like it. He's got no idea who it is yet. Probably best if you let us sell for you."

"I won't argue with that," Matt said. "But, anyway, let's not talk in here."

"OK," Ike said.

They wandered down to the clock tower, and stood alongside it.

Matt tugged at Ike's sleeve. "Let's talk while we walk."

Ike fell into step beside him. Soon they were on the pier amongst the other sightseers and fishermen. It brought back the times he used to go there fishing with his father. They used to catch everything from yellow-eyed mullet to rig shark and barracuda. They were good days.

He almost felt as if he were on board ship surrounded by the Pacific Ocean, high out of the water with salt wind buffeting his face.

"Can you drop the stuff off today?" Ike said as they got to the circular lookout at the seaward end of the pier.

Matt watched the fishermen. They had their rods hanging over the railings. "I'll have to organise it with BJ, but I'm sure it can be done." He looked south to the Port Hills, and thought they appeared deceptively close. They turned around and sauntered back towards the library complex bombarded by a raucous chorus from seagulls overhead.

"Good," Ike said. "We'll do it while the Sidewinders are distracted with the Kobe thing."

"OK, it's a done deal. We can forget any other meeting." Matt punched the air in exuberance. Just as fast he calmed down and watched New Brighton languish in the background. Assorted new and ramshackle buildings gave the place a quaint ambience. The pier had now become the main icon for Christchurch since the destruction of the Cathedral, and it had really put Brighton on the map.

Matt released a big sigh. This was all too easy. All he had to do was stand back and take the money. It was all good.

TWENTY-ONE

MATT TOOK the bag of marijuana out of the bottom drawer and put it into an old McDonald's paper bag he found on the workbench of BJ's father's garage. BJ held the door ajar. "Come on, Avery, let's get out of here."

Matt didn't have to be told. He was as anxious as BJ to get the stuff delivered to Joss and Ike and get it out of their possession. Let them take the risks from now on. He and BJ would simply pick up the cash and be invisible to the Sidewinders. They jumped into the truck and headed for the beach.

Joss and Ike were sitting on the swings in the children's playground when they arrived back at Brighton. They were in their usual black. The sky was dark and brooding, and there wasn't a breath of wind. It was that calm you get before a major storm. He had butterflies in his stomach. It was like the time when he had to give a talk on surfing in front of the whole school. Why he loved surfing. It was hard to put into words exactly why. How did you explain something that had to be experienced?

And now he had the same fear but it was heightened by the stakes. It might cost him and BJ their skins. But he was committed to helping his mum out, and he couldn't be seen as even a bigger loser in his father's eyes. He didn't have a choice. The best way to do the deal would be to march straight up to them like he was giving them a Big Mac burger. It would be so out in the open that even if the cops cruised by, they would just think they were delivering junk food. It was against his original plan. The same ruse would apply to the Sidewinders.

Matt and BJ parked the car and walked over to where Joss and Ike sat.

"I hope that's not burgers in that bag," Ike said from his swing.

"So do I." Joss twisted on her swing.

Ike patted his hip pocket. "I've got the grand."

"And I've got what you ordered." Matt handed the parcel to Ike, and Ike gave him a roll of cash in his closed fist.

"We'll let you know when the rest is sold." Ike peeked in the bag. "All good." I don't advise you to count the cash here, but it's all there."

"It better be." Matt's mouth tightened.

"Yeah," BJ said.

Ike gripped onto the bag. "By the way, Kobe's still in Christchurch Hospital. He's allowed visitors now."

"Cool." Matt turned to go. He was just in time to see and hear the Sidewinders rumble past on Marine Parade. They weren't stopping. But Matt doubted they would be going to visit Kobe.

"OK," Matt said to Ike and Joss. "Catch you later."

Matt punched BJ lightly on his upper arm. "Come on, Jolly, let's go and pay Kobe a visit."

"Do ya think it's safe?"

"Yup, why not?" I don't think we need worry about the Sidewinders."

"I hope you're right."

"We'll soon find out if he talked."

They got a park around the back of the hospital screened off by some native trees. Matt didn't want to be obvious if the Sidewinders did drift past.

Matt hated hospitals; there was always that antiseptic smell and the dry air-conditioned air. It brought on the same claustrophobic effect he got in an aeroplane, but this was firmly on the ground. When the automatic doors shut behind them it seemed to seal them off from the living, breathing world. He was terrified of ending up in a place like this with rows of hospital cots all connected up with tubes and 'state of the art' electronic stuff. It just made him plain jittery. They approached the nurse at the nurse's station and asked for Kobe. She was a woman in her thirties with short black hair and full bright-red lips. "Mr Jacobs is in number six just down the corridor." She pointed in that direction.

They got to room six and Matt could see Kobe through the window in the door. He was sleeping. Matt noticed severe bruising and lacerations on his face, and a patch of hair had been shaved on the right side of his head with a big scar that had been neatly sutured. The rest of his body outside of his hospital gown looked bruised but had no cuts or abrasions. They slipped in through the door. It squeaked and alerted Kobe. He wasn't sleeping at all. Matt supposed that was the result of being attacked by a gang of thugs and being afraid of their return.

They pulled up a chair alongside Kobe's bed. The hospital was in the central city, near the boatsheds on the Avon. Matt had a good view to the river and the Botanic Gardens below.

"Well," Kobe said. "You guys are a sight for sore eyes."

"And sore heads." Matt laughed.

"Well, enough of the jokes, eh. I'm not in a funny mood. And before you ask me, no, I did not drop you guys in it. But they are on the lookout for a red SUV."

"We know," BJ said and his gaze fell.

Kobe patted the scar on his head. "Have you any idea how many red SUVs there are around?"

"It doesn't look good." Matt folded his arms across his chest.

Kobe sat up in his bed and indicated for them to come in closer. "We have to be careful what we say around here. Just keep on denying it. They have no proof."

"They are outlaws," Matt said. "They don't need proof."

Kobe broke into a whisper. "You don't know Snake like I do. He likes to be sure he's got it right, and when he has, there's no stopping him."

"Don't give him any leads. It's too dangerous to sell any more weed."

"It's too late. I've already off-loaded to Ike and Joss to sell."

"Try to get it off the street. They'll trace it back to you. It's only a matter of time until they get back to the source."

"I'll see what I can do." Matt wiped the moisture off his brow with the back of his hand. He had a lucid moment. Off-loading the stuff to Ike and Joss was just plain stupid. They were too unreliable. His greed had shut his brain down. "This hospital air is crap," he said out of frustration.

BJ turned pale. "How you going to do that, Avery?"

"I don't know." Matt saw another problem. If he gave the money back to Ike, he would let down his mother by being unable to pay their bills. They would hit the wall without that money. Whatever he decided, it wasn't going to be easy.

A dark shadow filled the door. It was Sykes, the cop they had met before.

He spoke directly to Kobe. "Good to see you are wide awake now, Mr Jacobs. I wondered if your memory had returned."

"No, I'm afraid not, constable. It's still a blur."

"I'm sorry to hear that, son. It would be good to get those who did this to you." He turned to Matt and BJ. "Mr Avery and Mr Jolly, we meet again. I wonder if you two gentlemen can shed any light on this situation. Maybe you could assist us with our enquiries."

"I'm afraid not; this is all a big mystery to us. We are just visiting our friend."

"That's right," BJ said. "We gotta go now, right, Avery?"

"Right."

Matt stood up and led the way out of the hospital. In the car park the wind had come up and it had begun to rain. It blew cold on Matt's bare arms and face. They were soon in the Hilux and turning onto the road back to New Brighton via Bealey Avenue. They had just turned into Shirley Road when they heard the distinctive rumble of trouble. Matt looked behind and he saw Snake's angry face staring from underneath a German helmet. He wore a Driza-Bone coat. His hair and beard were blowing backwards and dripping water. Mullet and Barrel flanked him and the rest of the gang trailed behind them.

Snake and the other two overtook BJ, cut in front and waved him into the kerb. They parked in front of the Hilux with the others behind. Snake got off his bike and sauntered over to the open passenger side window where Matt was. He hunched his shoulders and screwed up his face against the splashes of rain. He cut straight to the chase. "You and your buddy and Kobe were seen in this vehicle out west with a payload of weed. Our weed." He grabbed Matt by the scruff of his T-shirt. "Whaddya say, rat?"

"It wasn't us; there are lots of trucks like this around."

"We'll see about that." He let Matt go with a jolt. The rain stopped briefly and a ray of sunshine blinked through. He walked around the outside of the truck and came back. He must have failed to see the two bullet holes in the tailgate due to the late-afternoon sun breaking through and shimmering on them, making them invisible.

He sidled back up to Matt's window. He looked him straight in the eye. "If I find out you're involved, you'll be history — not to mention that little hottie of yours. Get my drift, water rats?"

"Loud and clear," BJ said.

Matt was silent.

"OK, I'll be watchin' you closer than Uncle Sam."

With that, Snake wandered back to his bike. It burst into life with a dozen or so others and they were free to go for the present. Matt had to find Joss and Ike and see what he could do. He didn't even know where they lived. Where would they be on a Monday night with a McDonald's bag full of weed? "Let's go and find Joss and Ike," Matt said. "Head into the square; that's where some of his trade is, there and Manchester Street."

BJ started the truck and pointed it towards town to

the wipers clapping time like a metronome. The rain had given way to a fine drizzle, the type that slowly wets you through. They got a park in Cambridge Terrace and legged it into the square with the hoods of their jackets pulled up. The wet inner city pavements reflected the devastation. There was nothing but wasteland to the north. The Cathedral, especially, was a heartbreak in its present crumbling state, completely without tower or spire. It once epitomised the classic heritage of Christchurch and was now just a symbol of the power of destructive forces, like the whole CBD. Most of those 185 deaths in Christchurch were in two central city buildings, the CTV and PGC, but they were not in Cathedral Square.

"It looks like the main storm might have gone out to sea … I'm starving," Matt said. "Let's go and get a burger and fries. Might get a bit of groundswell out of it."

"Yeah, let's hope, some nice powerful big sets," BJ said. "No way we're gonna get a burger anywhere around here. We'll try over at Cathedral Junction. I haven't been there for ages."

Matt nodded. It was over that side most of their customers would hang out anyway.

They strode down the south side of the Cathedral, along a path barricaded off with half-round logs to protect the public from falling debris. They were flanked by tall derelict buildings with broken windows to their south. Matt watched a streetwalker approach a man. He didn't take up the offer. Matt had to admit she looked pretty raunchy in her micro mini and skintight sweater. The light rain didn't stop them.

Matt watched another girl, with pale skin and flaming orange lipstick, at the entrance to Cathedral Junction, and he saw a man walk up to her with something shiny in his hand. He only saw him from behind. He was skinny and dressed in black. Ten to one it was weed wrapped in tinfoil. And when he looked harder it was a fair bet. The man was Ike. Matt waited for them to do their business then went and ushered him out of earshot.

"So the thing is," Matt said, "I need the weed back."

"Too late for that; it's all sold already." Ike's hair hung in wet straggles, giving him the look of a long-haired pooch caught in the rain. "I've got the extra two grand at home ready for you. I had the stuff sold before you gave it to me."

It was a hell of a dilemma. He couldn't get the weed back, but he had three thousand bucks, fifteen hundred of which would go to BJ. He'd be able to pay his bills, woohoo, but how long would it be before the Sidewinders traced the weed back to them? In the meantime, he would go and get that burger.

TWENTY-TWO

MATT LAY in bed thinking about the trouble he was in. The sun sneaked through the gaps in the curtains, so he hopped out of bed and threw them open and clinked the empty beer bottles on the sill as he did. He jumped back into bed. Ah, that was better! Now he could feel the warmth of the sun on his whole body. He looked around the room at a week's worth of dirty clothes scattered on the floor where he had climbed out of them. They gave the room a musty, closed-in smell. His mother was trying to train him to do his own washing, but she wasn't having much luck. He knew she would give up in disgust and do it long before he did. The sun shone through the bottles, creating amber patterns on the wall opposite. They amused him, the way they danced on the wallpaper like tiny ballerinas. They made him think of Kristy for a moment, but then he returned to the here and now. He really had to clean this room up some time, but it wouldn't be today. He lay back and took a cigarette out of the packet he had snatched from the bedside cabinet. He lit it, and sucked in a lungful.

Things were heating up in more ways than one, but he was determined to keep his life as close to normal as possible. He sucked in another big dollop of smoke. He would go and see about glassing his board today, but maybe he would text Kristy and see what she was up to first. He went warm inside every time he thought of her. Let the Sidewinders do their worst; he and BJ would be safe for now. They would only trace the weed back to Ike and Joss and they had their alibis ready — the primo stuff came from a contact up north. They just had to keep their nerve. He was a little bit worried about BJ in that respect, but at least he clammed up under pressure and wasn't the type to go shooting his mouth off.

Matt finished his smoke and stubbed it out in the paua shell ashtray. He pulled back the covers, sprang out of bed and slid into jeans and black T-shirt that he retrieved from the floor. The smell of fried bacon hit him as soon as he opened his bedroom door. He walked through the living room to where his mother was bent over the stove. She wore a pink leisure suit, which made her look quite youthful from the back. Matt leaned over by her side and took a big whiff.

"Smells great."

"Just hold your whist. It'll be ready in a moment." She turned to look at him. "Put some toast in, will you?"

"Sure." He shoved the bread into the toaster slot and pushed the lever down. It soon popped. He placed the two slices of toast on his plate on the bench. "I've got great news."

She looked him in the eyes to show he had her

attention. "I can take any amount of good news. What is it?" She slid the eggs out of the pan onto the toast on his plate.

"Yeah. OK, the news. I made fifteen hundred bucks in commission this last fortnight. Jack was real chuffed with my sales."

"Oh, that's wonderful. If only your father knew that."

"I'm not worried about him, but at least we are paying our own way."

"I'm proud of you, dear."

"We don't need him, that's for sure."

His mother beamed. "I can't wait to tell Jude at work. She's always singing the praises of her son who sells insurance."

Matt went red in the face. "No need to go overboard, Mum."

"I want to! Why shouldn't I celebrate your success?"

Matt took his plate to the table and grabbed a knife and fork on the way. His mother sat at the opposite end nursing a coffee. He dug into his bacon and eggs, and smacked his lips.

"What are you doing today, dear?" His mother put her coffee on the table in front of her.

"I'm going to catch up with Kristy, and then I'll be working on my board."

Matt finished his breakfast and then texted Kristy to meet him at the Pier Café. He was on foot today because BJ was busy detailing cars for his father. What he would give for a set of his own wheels.

Kristy sat at a table with a view of the beach. Matt walked over and pulled up a chair opposite her. She looked beautiful with her soft green eyes and sun-bleached hair that framed her little turned-up nose and full red lips. He couldn't believe she was his girlfriend. How did he get so lucky? She was a knockout in her little pink T-shirt and blue jeans.

"I enjoyed Sunday night," Kristy said. "Nothing against BJ but it was good to get some together time."

Matt nonchalantly watched the traffic going down Marine Parade. Some motorbikes appeared. He sat upright. "What did you say?"

"I was talking about the other night."

He breathed easy. "Oh, OK." It was a group of older guys suffering from a midlife crisis or something. They were the harmless type of biker, anyway.

Kristy sipped her coffee then put her cup down on the table. "How is your friend who got beaten up?"

"They think he will live," Matt said. "He's not really a friend."

"Oh well, I hope they get who did it."

"So do I," Matt said. "But let's not obsess. It's so cool just being with you again … How's work?"

"You know. Rick's still impossible, but I'll be back at uni soon."

"I don't know how you put up with that little fascist."

Kristy sipped from her cup and put it down again.

"How are the surfboard sales? By the way, I saw your boss, Jack, in the mall."

"That's cool. I've just sold fifteen hundred bucks' worth. What did he say?" Matt grinned.

Kristy raised her cup. "I just told him how pleased I was about your job. Here's to the best surfboard salesman in New Brighton."

"I wouldn't say that."

"I would … he was just pleased for you," Kristy said. "You've got to learn not to be so modest."

"Did he say anything else?"

"No, nothing."

Matt caught the dark shape of a person flash by from the direction of the pier and felt a sinking sensation in his chest. By the time he realised who it was, she was already approaching their table. Joss stuck out like a female Darth Vader.

She ignored Kristy, leaned on the table and looked hard into Matt's eyes. "Do you have a moment to talk? It's urgent."

Matt flushed and turned to Kristy. "Sorry, do you mind? It's work."

Kristy raised her eyebrows. "No, go right ahead."

"Be back in a moment." He and Joss stepped aside to talk in private. Matt looked for any clues on her face as to what was on her mind, but her eyes were blank. "What was it you wanted?" he said.

"I think the shit is about to hit the fan," Joss said.

"Why? Is it the Sidewinders?"

"You could say that. They've started to rough up our customers." Her eyes looked down. "But none have given anything away, as far as we know. But if they start bribing them with freebee joints, we might be in trouble."

"Don't like the sound of that."

"Well, don't worry. They won't get anything out of us. We are sticking to our story. They have no proof."

"That's good but I can't help feeling bad about it."

"Don't! We'll ride it out."

"Anyway, thanks for the warning."

"If I were you I would get those bullet holes in the back of BJ's truck filled before they discover them. They are still on about a red SUV. Those holes are a dead giveaway."

"OK, thanks," Matt said. "Keep us in the loop."

Joss left and Matt wandered back to his table.

"That must have been pretty intense business," Kristy said.

"Oh yeah, I sold her a board for her boyfriend. He wants some modifications done to the fins."

"Oh, I see."

"Anyway, speaking of work, I've gotta go and catch up on my paperwork."

"Wish you didn't have to go. We have hardly talked, and you didn't have anything to eat.

"We'll catch up soon."

Matt left her to sit. She looked alone and abandoned, and, as he walked, he texted BJ. Get those bloody bullet holes filled in before the Sidewinders fill us in. Then he walked to Jack's factory as if his shoes were filled with lead.

Matt didn't see Jack in his office, so he went out to the glassing bays. Jack was standing by a worker showing him how to apply cloth and resin to what Matt thought was going to be a sexy little board. He waited for Jack to finish showing the guy and then he went over.

"I thought today might be a good day for glassing the board."

Jack led him out of the bay and looked him in the face, but Matt had not seen that tired faraway look before in his eyes. The pressure of work must have been getting to him. Jack grunted a reply. "Today's not a good day. It's nearly lunch time, and it would be pushing it to do your board today: we are talking days to glass a board. I'm flat out and I haven't got a bay free. Besides, I need to keep an eye on you."

Matt stepped back. "OK." This wasn't like Jack at all.

Just as quickly, the wild look went out of his eye and his voice calmed.

"Come into my office and we'll talk."

They both pulled up a chair in the office facing each other in a fashion that had almost become a ritual with them.

"I'll get straight to the point," Jack said. "I have it on

good authority that you are selling surfboards for me."

"Well … it was sort of a little white lie for my girlfriend to think I had a job."

"I know. I ran into her down the mall. And she couldn't wait to tell me how much you enjoyed it. Don't worry, I didn't ruin your little game, but I was sorely tempted."

"I'm sorry," Matt said. "I just wanted to stay in good with her — you know, impress her. I didn't want her to know I'm unemployed."

Jack shifted in his chair. "That's not exactly true either, is it? I did the maths and came to the conclusion your association with Kobe is about selling drugs."

"Well … sort of."

"What do you mean sort of?" His mouth flattened out.

"I'm not selling them any more. I've off-loaded them."

"I'm assuming they paid you for them." Jack crossed his arms and legs. "I'm sorry, Matt. I like you, and I think you may have potential as a board shaper. But I can't bring my firm into bad repute by having an association with those who push illegal substances."

"Well, I'm not doing it now."

"You are still living off that illicit money. I'm not that big a fool." Jack uncrossed his arms. "Come back and talk when you've straightened yourself out. There could be a lot of export work in the pipeline, so that apprenticeship could happen." Matt's heart sank in his chest. This was the absolute pits. Talk about the best of times and the worst of times. Not only was he and his two best friends in danger from the Sidewinders, but the only job he ever wanted and cared about hung in the balance.

TWENTY-THREE

MATT AND BJ leaned against the sea wall at the Brighton Ramp. Matt looked at the afternoon sky. It was slate grey and the clouds churned like some sort of witch's brew. There were distant claps of thunder and the occasional stab of lightning from sky to sea, well out. He scoped the waves. It was not a good day for surfing. Some big sets rolled in, and, when they hit the sand banks that ran the length of the beach, they closed out and turned the inshore break into a dirty brown mess. Fresh piles of seaweed lay scattered between the water's edge and the high-tide mark. He could smell their iodine stench.

"What say we brave the conditions and go for a surf?" BJ said to Matt.

"Not today, buddy. I value my goolies too highly for that, even if the waves are super gnarly out the back."

Matt pulled up his hood against the bitter wind. He knew it would be a challenge to get out there. They must have been over head-height. The sea roared in his ears like an angry beast. The bleak conditions did not stop the dedicated beachcombers, who seemed to move like ghosts along the foreshore. It was one of those summer days that was more like winter.

"It's a miserable bloody day. I feel frozen and made of lead," Matt said. The windblown sand swirled along the foreshore and stung his face. He fought to keep it out of his eyes; even the usually noisy gulls just hovered quietly, buffeted by the winds.

BJ turned to Matt. "If you're fretting over the Sidewinders, I can get the guys at the old man's paint shop to take care of the bullet holes in the Hilux."

"Cool." Matt slapped BJ on the shoulder and was silent.

The atmosphere hung heavy.

"Yeah, they match the paint so well there's nothing to see."

Something bad was going down.

A voice said softly, "Hey, you guys." Joss jumped down from the Ramp car park onto the sand and faced them. "Bad news." Her hair was jet black against her pale skin, and her dark-brown eyes were wild. "The Sidewinders know you guys stole their weed."

"Ya shitting me!" Matt's heavy heart turned to fire, and the blood rose in his veins.

BJ went suddenly pale. "I'm scared, Avery, very scared. What are we going to do?"

Matt's face was red. "I need time to think. How could this happen? I thought you were going to stick to your story."

"We were," Joss said. "That was until they threatened Ike's elderly parents. He caved in like a sandcastle hit by the incoming tide."

"Yeah, that's just great. He's sacrificed us." Matt gnawed his nails.

"Well, at least you've got some warning. Get out of here and stay low for a while."

"We can do that but they won't forget, and then there's Kristy to worry about."

"Warn her then disappear."

Matt wiped his forehead with his hand. "We need to take her with us."

"What about her olds?" BJ said.

"I'll leave you to it." Joss left as fast as she arrived.

BJ grabbed Matt's bicep fiercely and said, "Hey I've got an idea. We can all hide out at our bach at Taylors."

"Cool. I'll tell Mum it's a work trip. You can sweet-talk your olds, and we'll tell Kristy the surf's so much better over there. She can tell her olds she's with a girlfriend. It's sorted."

But in the meantime it was time to make a discreet exit before the Sidewinders discovered the Hilux parked out on the Parade. They had just got in the cab of the Hilux when there was a tap on the window. Matt jumped so high he nearly hit his head on the roof.

He had a big picture of Snake coming at him, teeth bared and knuckles clenched, with his henchmen behind him. It was a big relief when he turned to see the rugged features of Ben Burrows.

He put the window down. Burrow's brow was

wrinkled. "I'm surprised to see you guys so out in the open. The Sidewinders are on to you."

"We know," Matt said. "We were just about to disappear."

"Well," Burrows said, "you might want to rethink that."

Matt scratched his head. "Why's that?"

Burrows stood with his legs apart, shifting his weight from one to another, and his head filled the window. "Well, it's like this. I was coming back from town, and I saw the Sidewinders turning into their HQ with your little lady on the back of the ute. She had a goon either side of her. Her hair was a shambles. She looked pale and terrified. I'm thinking maybe it's a job for the cops."

"Shit! I don't believe it! We can't bring the cops into it … too much to lose." Matt turned to get BJ's response. "Eh, BJ?"

"Maybe he's talking sense." BJ was pale, which seemed to emphasise the freckles around his nose and chubby cheeks.

"No way. I got her into this, and I'm gonna get her out of it."

"You mean we, don't you, Avery?" "Well, yeah, I guess."

"I'd like to help, guys," Burrows said, "but I think it's best left to the cops. You don't know what they are like."

"We aren't going to take them on; we are going to outsmart them," Matt said.

"Good luck with that," Burrows said, and dawdled over to the beach.

It was shitty news. There was no way they were any sort of physical match for the Sidewinders. He was going to have to get inside the gang's HQ and rescue Kristy. It wasn't going to be easy. Then once he got her out they could escape to BJ's bach and wait for the heat to die down.

Matt said, "Let's hit the Sidewinders' HQ, now!"

"I still think we should call the cops," BJ replied.

"Then what? Everybody learns about our drug dealing, and we become young crims?"

"At least we would all be alive."

"It won't come to that."

There was nothing much between Brighton and Marshlands, where the gang's headquarters were, just street after street of houses, driveways and shrubby front gardens, and the odd open paddock. To Matt it all went past in a blur. His mind was on what he was going to do when he got there. He was going to have to think on his feet. He wasn't bad at doing that, after all the shit he had been through in the last couple of months. But he certainly wasn't going to underestimate the Sidewinders.

The headquarters were off a busy through-road between Marshlands and Redwood. When they got within a block of the headquarters, Matt told BJ to pull over behind some poplar and sycamore trees. He remembered those trees from the playground at school. The kids had called them helicopter trees. This was because the seed had a wing attached and when it was thrown in the air it spun like helicopter blades all the way to the ground. It never failed to amaze him the silly associations he made with things when he was under pressure. He guessed it was anything to take his mind off what looked like impending doom.

From where they were parked, Matt could see the two-metre block fence topped with razor wire, and a closed-circuit TV camera protruded from the house. He hatched a plan with BJ as they sat in the truck watching.

"OK, this is what we are going to do."

"What?" BJ said.

"I'll throw a rock at the camera, which will hopefully shut it down and get the Sidewinders to give chase." He scratched his chin. "The gate will be left open while the gang exit." Well, he hoped. "I'll hide behind one of those broad-trunked sycamore trees while they roar off after you and the Hilux."

"And then what — I get caught?"

"You'll be far enough ahead to lose them."

"Sounds all right in theory."

"When all the heat has died down, come back later. Park down the road and wait for me and Kristy, and we will escape to the bach."

BJ started the Hilux and parked in front of the headquarters. Matt got out and picked up a rock from a few strewn on a pile of sand out in front. It looked like a pile left over from some concreting work. He threw it at the camera. It made contact with a loud crack. He jumped into the truck and BJ took off. There was a combined snarl of motorbikes starting. BJ stopped the truck and let him out down the road to hide until all was clear. They made sure they were out of camera range, in case it was still working. Matt hid behind a tree large enough to hide his trim body.

He would have to move around the trunk to stay out of view. BJ was nearly out of sight by the time the first motorbike came through the gate. About a dozen of them gave chase. The whole road came alive with the thunderous roars of a dozen or so motorcycles … and to think they were all chasing poor old BJ. He hoped like hell they didn't catch him. The motorcycles sounded angry, which went with the looks on the bikers' faces. Their hair and beards were flying out behind them, no time for helmets.

Matt thought there would probably only be a couple of them looking after Kristy. From where he stood he could see there was nobody in the turret on top of the house, but there was a guy at the gate, and it was Stretch. His skinniness and height was a giveaway. They all tended to look the same in their oil-stained jeans and cut-off jackets and with the Sidewinder snake in striking mode, painted on their patches in black and red. But that was another reason why Matt knew it was Stretch. He didn't have a patch or a beard. It looked as though the prospect had been left behind. Maybe they didn't need him to catch BJ. That would be kudos for the patched guys.

The fact that Stretch was at the gate suggested that the camera was out. How the hell was he going to get past him? He didn't have to wait long. There was a shout from down the drive and Stretch went running to the source of it. Matt crept along the fence line until he came to the gate and then peered down the drive and up to the turret. There was no one around. He crossed his fingers and toes that the camera wasn't working, or that they weren't watching the monitor at that moment, if it was still working.

He made a dash for safety and dived beneath the front windows. He would now be out of view from those inside the house and from the camera. He waited a few minutes and crept around the north side of the house, which was really only a path about a metre wide: weatherboards and windows one side, solid block wall the other. He had to keep low to be below the window level. He crept along on all fours along the muddy path fringed with some large-leafed ivy. So far, so good. There was no hint of discovery. He came out at what looked like the toilet block. It had louvred windows and an old breather pipe up the wall with a meshed dome on it.

He shimmied around the toilet and noticed a Doberman in a cage down the back of the section. He didn't know how it managed it, but it was fast asleep. He poked his head around the corner of the toilet block, and he was looking at the deck and a lounge area that opened out to a courtyard with two motorcycles parked on it. It was eerie. There was no one around. They must be in guarding Kristy. He was very aware the others could return at any time.

He had to be in and out. He made a run through the sliding doors into the bar with all the drinks on the table where the guys had left them. There were a lot of posters of bare-breasted women, big bikes and hairy men on the walls. A confederate flag hung at the back of the bar. He stood behind the door between the bar and the rest of the house. He could hear two men talking in the hallway; it sounded like Snake and Mullet.

"I'll go and ring someone about getting a new camera. You and Stretch go upstairs and keep an eye out."

"OK, boss. The girl's not going anywhere."

Once they had gone, Matt slid into the hallway. One of the hallway doors was slightly open and he could see Kristy tied to a chair. He took in a deep breath and opened the door. He shut it behind him.

Kristy's eyes were red and her eyeliner had smudged. She didn't look like Kristy at all. Her hair was all over the place.

She whispered, "Oh Matt, I'm so scared." She sobbed, "Get me out of here … please."

"That's what I aim to do. I'm so sorry."

"No time; just get me out."

Matt undid her ropes as fast as he could. He stood up, hauled Kristy to her feet and headed for the door.

"Going somewhere, arsehole?" Snake's huge frame blotted out the sunlight. He grabbed Matt and pushed his arm up his back. He was too strong for him to repel his grip. "I thought she would be good bait," Snake snarled.

"Run for it, Kristy!" Matt shouted. Kristy sprinted down the driveway, but the Sidewinders were now back. Barrel skidded his bike to a halt in front of her, and she cannoned into it. He reached out and wrapped his arm around her waist. "Very tasty," he sneered.

The good news, if there was any to be had, was that BJ had got away. Matt watched them bring Kristy back to Snake. His heart sank. How could they possibly escape now?

TWENTY-FOUR

BJ WATCHED the bikers' entourage stop. Mullet got out and opened the double wooden gates that had just about fallen over. They turned off onto a sandy stretch of land that ran alongside the pines, ringed by gorse. Once they got well in they would be difficult to see from the road. He was far enough back that he hoped they wouldn't notice him. The light was starting to fade over the pines as the Sidewinders' tail-lights disappeared into the early-evening shadows. They were not far from the headwaters of the Waimakariri River. He ran a hand over his clammy T-shirt. He wound the window down for relief, and could smell the fresh pine fragrance on the breeze mixed with his sweat. He sat back and lit up a smoke.

It might have been quite pleasant under different circumstances. He drew long and hard on the smoke. What was the best strategy? It was a no-brainer: get the cops … they would probably only get diversion as they were only sixteen, but would soon be seventeen. He reckoned that was the answer. Ben Burrows was right. But he doubted Matt would ever understand. Then the Hilux lit up as if by magic. A car had pulled up behind him with its lights on full beam. The panic rose in him like the time a rogue wave dumped on him and held him under a long time.

The lights went out and a door slammed. There was the clack of footsteps on the road and the passenger door clicked and opened. BJ tensed up, then breathed easy. "Oh, hello, Mr Avery. I thought you were more bikers."

Matt's father talked through the open door. "And why would you be worried about them?"

BJ threw his cigarette butt out the window. "No reason."

"I was looking for Matt." He had one arm on the roof and peered in.

BJ took a deep breath. "It was a long shot you would find him here."

"I have just been to Spencer Park. I know you guys hang out around there sometimes. I checked out just about everywhere else."

BJ leaned towards him. "Not lately, though." He cleared his throat. "Matt and Kristy have been taken by the Sidewinders."

"Why? Where are they?"

"We sort of … owe them money. They are up that track by the plantation." BJ pointed in the general direction.

"Well, I'm going in. You coming?"

"I think we should get the cops," BJ said. His voice quavered.

"Not necessary, BJ," he said. "At their core the

Sidewinders are businessmen, and I understand businessmen. I'm sure I'll be able to come to an amicable arrangement with them if I wave a bit of moolah around."

"You don't know them," BJ said.

"See if I'm right, come on." Matt's father snatched a torch from the boot of his XK Jaguar, and the duo marched off together down the clearing in the direction of the shouting and yahooing.

The ropes bit into Matt's wrists. They were tied behind his back. He sat beside Kristy on the tray of the ute with their backs to the cab. "Hey, how about taking these things off?" he said to Snake.

"OK," he replied, "but if you try to make a run for it, you're dead."

"We won't," Matt said. He could see it in Kristy's eyes that she wondered what fate they had in store for her. And they wouldn't have to wait very long. He lifted his gaze over to where some of the lower-ranked bikers were gathering firewood for a bonfire they were going to party around later. They were in an area near a sort of shallow amphitheatre surrounded by gorse. It was unlikely they could be seen from the road, so not much chance some civic-minded citizen would ring the fire department, even though this was a fire-ban area.

The biker named Barrel, which was short for Barrel Guts, was already pawing Kristy and he said, "Guess what, sweetie? You're on the block tonight."

Matt knew that was biker talk for gang rape.

"I look forward to that," said another greasy-haired biker and threw him a can of lager.

Matt slid over the side of the ute while Snake lifted the tailgate down so Kristy could get out. The ute was parked in a clearing that backed onto a small area of pine trees. Snake motioned them over to where the other bikers had piled up branches in the hollow. They stood at the edge of an old bonfire site, one they had no doubt used before. The area was littered with used beer bottles, squashed cans and charcoaled pine branches.

Matt was determined he would hang tough till the end. He was just so bummed that he was powerless to help Kristy. He had got her into this mess, but how would he get her out? The whole place smelled of stale urine and ashes and it made him sick to his stomach. He placed his hand on her shoulder to try to reassure her. She shrugged it off. He caught her gaze, but she shivered and wouldn't meet his eyes. The fire was going now. Snake had emptied a few litres of petrol over it and it had exploded into life.

Matt stood in front of the fire with Mullet, one of the ugliest, toughest-looking guys, standing guard over him. Matt soaked up the raw heat. Now they started to maul Kristy. He was bloody useless; just had to stand and watch it happen. Barrel grinned and tore her blouse off, then her jeans. He couldn't bear to see Kristy pulled to the ground and raped; he turned his head and stared into the darkness down the dirt track.

What the hell … was that a flashlight? It was! Someone was coming at a trot; the torchlight flickered on the prickly gorse. It could only be BJ, as good as nobody. Couldn't be the cops; they would come in sirens blaring. Still, it was a distraction. The bikers obviously hadn't noticed. He spun back to see Barrel trying to grapple a near-naked Kristy to the ground. "Hey, cops!" he screamed at the top of his lungs. "The cops are coming!" He pointed down the lane. Barrel stopped dead and stared.

It didn't take Snake long to suss it out. "Bullshit," he said, and cuffed Matt around the ear. "Some stupid fucker with a torch."

Well, two, actually. It was BJ and his own father. His father marched straight up to Snake. " Matt's my son. Let them all go. What have they ever done to you?" It was the only time Matt had ever seen him bare his teeth. The biker's attention turned from Kristy to his father, who took off his jacket and wrapped it around Kristy's shoulders.

"So you don't know," Snake said. "Your boy stole from us." He grinned, showing uneven tobacco-stained teeth.

"What did he steal?"

Snake fondled the knife on his belt. "Weed."

"What does he owe you?"Snake took the knife off his belt and held it high. He tapped Matt under the chin with it. "The small sum of fifty thousand dollars. Ain't that right, boy? Tell Daddy the truth now."

"I'll see you get it back," Matt's father said and looked for a response from Matt's direction but didn't get it.

Snake holstered the knife. "It's too easy. We'll get it back — but first our honour must be avenged."

"How?" Matt's father's mouth dropped and his brow wrinkled.

Snake smiled. "This little shit has to learn his lesson, take a bit of punishment. We put his mate in hospital."

"I can pay," Matt's father said and he pulled out his phone. "I'm calling the police."

"Don't be stupid … You'll pay, all right." Snake hit him full in the face and knocked him backwards. "Take them away and tie them up. We'll deal to them later," he said to Mullet. He snatched the phone and crunched it under his boot heel.

Mullet took them away to the small clearing near the ute and tied them back to back to a couple of random pine trees. BJ and Kristy were tied up together and so were Matt and his father. This was the only way Matt would breathe the same air as his father. What did his old man think he was doing? Did he think the Sidewinders shared some sort of businessman's code? They were outlaws. His only real concern for the moment was Kristy. If they were not rescued she was going to be raped and then what? And it was all down to him. And what about poor old BJ who had followed him faithfully? It would be curtains for him too. It didn't matter about himself or the old man. They had been the cause of this.

He yelled out, "You all right, Kristy?"

"No!" came the jittery reply.

He yelled out to BJ.

"I'm not OK either, Avery!"

What the hell could he do? He tested the ropes on his hands and there was no give at all. They weren't going to be rescued, that was for sure.

He watched the Sidewinders through small gaps in the gorse, and the firelight caused a strobe light effect on them. They danced around the blazing fire, drinking from cans of beer and whooping and hollering like Shawnee Indians on the warpath. He wriggled his arms behind him but they were tied tight and the more he wriggled the more they bit into his flesh. The gorse was thick on the road side and he knew they couldn't be seen from there.

"This is all down to you!" Matt shouted to his father on the other side of the tree.

"You think so? I don't remember stealing fifty thousand dollars' worth of drugs."

"You started it all by walking out on us."

"I'm sorry. I tried my best but my marriage just fizzled."

"Yeah, well, that didn't mean you had to be a bastard to me."

"Life's not always that simple … I may have walked

out on your mother, but I didn't walk out on you. In retrospect, maybe I was misguided."

He wasn't telling Matt anything he didn't already know, but it was the first time he had ever heard his father admit it. He guessed that was something. And before he knew it, he was talking back.

"You are right about that," Matt said.

"Your mother and I had just come to a natural end, but I still respect her." There was a croak in his voice. "But you and I are different. I only wanted to make my business a success for you. So one day you would have financial independence. And I wouldn't have to worry about you any more."

Matt felt his anger lose its impetus. "You didn't give me a fair go."

"Yes." His father cleared his throat. "I'm beginning to see that now."

"I always wanted to be a board shaper. You can make mega dollars at that — look at Jack Dawson."

"I know. I bumped into him at the Pier Café the other day and he said you have a lot of natural talent. He reckons you got it from me."

Matt coughed. "Don't know about that. Maybe I got it from Mum."

"Well, that's very possible."

Matt pulled on his ropes; still no movement.

He watched the bonfire. The bikers were still dancing around, drinking and working themselves up to indulge in whatever atrocities crossed their mind. He had heard about the notorious exploits of the Sidewinders from the Burrows brothers, the vicious rapes and the sudden disappearances and horrendous murders of their adversaries.

The higher-up members of the gang never got to court because the lowliest members, the prospects, took the rap for them. This was all part of the ritual they had to go through to become a fully-patched member of the gang. He despaired to think of any harm coming to his beautiful Kristy and to think it was all pretty much fuelled by his hatred of his father, who was now going to suffer the same fate as him. It was all too silly for words.

Mullet came over to them and checked their ropes. "Got any last requests?" He grinned like a Doberman.

"Yes, let us go, you barbarian," Matt said.

"It will take more than big words to save you now, suckers." Satisfied they weren't going anywhere, Mullet went back to the freaks around the bonfire. Matt watched them party. He could hear BJ and Kristy talking in hushed voices, but he couldn't hear what they were saying.

His father broke in. "I don't know if we are going to get out of here, but if we do, can you give me another chance?"

"Let's get out of here first, all right?" Matt said. And he wondered how they were going to do it. The immediate future looked grim. If only he could get loose and untie the others, maybe they could slink away into the trees. They didn't have a sentry at the moment. He felt his father's fingers brush his wrist, and it brought the futility of the situation back. Just when he thought things were settling down, he saw Snake's sinister form approach. He had his knife unsheathed but his features were difficult to make out. Matt wriggled his hands in desperation but the ropes held tight. Snake was soon eyeball to eyeball with him. He could smell his alcohol-laden, smoky breath. Snake held the knife to his neck, which made him wince. The cold steel bit into his clammy flesh and he thought he was going to die.

"Where are the drugs?" Snake said.

Matt did some quick thinking. "Buried in the sand hills at North Beach."

Snake took the pressure off the knife and sheathed it. "So you've bought some time, that's all. You're going to show us where they are and then you're gonna die. We'll make a job of it this time, not like with your rat mate Kobe." He spat in his face then walked away into the brush. Matt tried again to loosen his hands but it was hopeless. His hands were tied to his father's round the tree. He whispered to his father, "Hey, Dad, I've got an idea. The trunk of this tree narrows slightly as it goes up. If we both stand up together maybe the tension will slacken off and we might be able to pick ourselves loose."

His father coughed. "Anything is worth a try." They

stood and wriggled their backs slowly up the trunk, and, as he'd hoped, the pressure went off. Matt could feel where the knot was. It was just a big reef knot so he moved his hands until it slackened a bit. They were in luck; there was a small piece of branch, broken off, that stuck out from the trunk like a finger. Matt shoved the branch into the centre of the knot and worked it loose. From there, it just undid and he slid his hands free.

"Right, nice work," his father said, as he tackled the knots on his father's wrist. He heard a twig crack behind him. He jerked his head around in time to see the branch that Snake was swinging at him. Then everything went black.

BJ saw him go down and now he lay so still. "You've killed him," he yelled.

Matt's father said, "What have you done?"

"Let him die! BJ knows where the drugs are," Snake snarled, as he tied Matt's father to the tree again.

BJ had been watching Matt for vital signs and soon Matt's body began to twitch and unfurl from his previous foetal position, slow at first but then there was a strengthening of movement in his arms and legs. He was alive. Snake had left him for dead and gone back to the bonfire.

"He looks terrible!" said Matt's father.

"Yeah," BJ said, "but he's alive."

"Thank God for that," Kristy shouted from the far

side of her tree. "But how are we going to get out of here now?"

"I don't know," BJ said.

"You should have called the cops when you had an opportunity," Kristy said.

"Hindsight's twenty-twenty," BJ replied.

"She's right," said Matt's father, "it was my fault. I thought I could reason with them, but I didn't know about your drug involvement."

Snake arrived back. Matt lay still and looked dead. Snake gave him a good kick in the backside to see if he was still alive. Matt's reaction was instinctive. He grabbed Snake's leg and twisted it so hard the biker had no option but to hit the ground. But Snake was soon on his feet and faced Matt who was now standing as well. He pulled his knife from his sheath. "You're dead meat, surfer boy."

"You reckon?" Matt placed his arms in a blocking position to protect his chest and lower body.

"You're gonna pay. Nobody steals from us." He lunged forward with his knife extended.

Matt stepped back. "Heard you before."

BJ looked on helpless as Snake lunged again. Matt blocked and stepped back, and then raised his right leg into a roundhouse kick that slammed down hard on the side of Snake's bearded face. He fell to the ground, cold. BJ looked around him and over to the bonfire. Nobody had missed Snake or seen what was going on. They were making so much noise drinking around the fire that they hadn't heard a thing and it was dark outside the fire circle. Matt left Snake lying, grabbed the knife and cut everybody free. Now they just had to get out of there.

Their luck had changed. Matt saw that the keys had been left in the bikers' ute. BJ and Kristy jumped on the back and Matt and his father got in the front, Matt in the driver's seat. The big V8 throbbed into life and it immediately attracted attention from the bonfire crew. Matt threw it into reverse and then spun around to face the road. The dancing stopped and there was a mad scuttle for motorbikes. He gunned it, and watched the pursuers backlit by the fire in his rear-view mirror. Everything was in slow motion — the way they kicked their big bikes into action and slid sideways down the sandy track in hot pursuit. Several bikers had discovered Snake and were helping him to his feet. Matt floored it, but it wasn't easy dodging holes and overhanging gorse.

Six of them had taken off after them. By the time they hit the Main North Road, the bikers were gaining on them. Luck favoured Matt, and he made it into the traffic flow that blocked the bikers' way out of Kainga Road. He flashed through Chaney's Corner onto Marshlands Road overtaking everything in sight.

Matt was well ahead now and turned left into Prestons Road, but they caught up with him coming onto Mairehau Road. He accelerated hard, and a space opened up. Damn! He should have gone to the Shirley cop shop. But he wanted to hand them over to Wilson and Sykes, the cops that had been bugging them.

"You're going the long way round; you could have shot down Bower Ave," his father said as they bumped and thumped down the fractured mess that was Beach Road.

"Yeah, I thought that's what they would do, if we got far enough ahead."

But his ruse didn't work. They were on to them now. Their headlights spotlighted the ute. Mullet caught up and came alongside and shouted to Kristy and BJ on the back, "You're dead, grommets." Barrel came level with Matt's window and there was a dull thwack! thwack! as he smashed it with an old motorcycle chain that he had worn draped across his chest like the cartridge belt on a Mexican bandit. The window shattered and caved in all over Matt's shoulders. He shook it off.

He swerved into Barrel and sent his bike and the other beside him sliding into the middle of the road on their sides, with cars dodging them from both directions. Two other bikers stopped to help them while Mullet and another with a long flowing beard continued the chase. Matt raced on towards the New Brighton police station. BJ and Kristy were lying down in the back to avoid being lashed by a biker's chain.

Matt gunned it, but so did they. Sweat beaded on his brow and his breathing was rapid. He would welcome the cops now. "They'll get theirs," he said to his father, "for what they did to Kristy." Matt wiped the sweat off his brow with the back of his hand. His father's eyebrows were knitted over his grey eyes. "I'm all for getting the cops. I'd sooner you risk some sort of charge than you three lose your lives. Your mother would understand."

"I reckon you're right, Dad."

The bikers clung tight to the tailgate. Without warning, Matt hit the brakes. He hoped Kristy and BJ would be OK with the sudden stop. There were too huge thuds. A jolt of pain ran up the back of his neck. The whole ute shuddered and the glove box fell open and he saw a handgun and a plastic bag of white crystalline powder. It looked about 500 grams or so. The gun was an old school Colt revolver, but there were no bullets in the chamber.

"Don't pick it up!" Matt yelled. "You don't want your prints all over that. The cops may be able to tie it to a murder." His father gulped and nodded. Matt looked into his rear-view mirror. The bikers had smashed into the tailgate. He snatched a quick glance through the rear window. Bikes and riders lay spread-eagled across Beach Road. They weren't going anywhere.

Further up the road he stopped and checked to see how BJ and Kristy were. They were bruised and a bit shaken up, cold and windblown. They were sitting on some pieces of four by two to protect their butts from the cold metal tray. They were just about there. Matt jumped back into the ute and buried his foot. He looked in the rear-vision mirror just in time to see other bikers arrive to help the fallen ones. Stretch and another prospect gave chase. Matt knew the stakes were higher now. They could add half a kilo of methamphetamine to the debt they already owed the Sidewinders. If these prospects could catch them, or at least get their meth back, that would be worth a patch to them. They passed two ambulances on the way with lights flashing and sirens wailing while they hightailed it into the night.

Every move they made, the prospects were stuck right behind them like superglue, their headlights boring into his rear-vision mirror. Matt thought of braking hard again but they were hanging back just far enough not to fall for that one again. They hit Marine Parade. Halfway down that straight, right opposite the North Beach Memorial Hall, Stretch overtook and pulled in front of them. Matt tried to run him down but he managed to stay just ahead. The other biker pulled level with the driver's door, then suddenly accelerated ahead and, taking a beer bottle from his cut-off jacket pocket, threw it over his left shoulder. Boof! It was a bull's-eye, smack in the middle of their windscreen. They were nearly in Brighton. The smell of beer filled the cab. It made Matt sneeze and at the same time he couldn't see a thing. It was a glass whiteout. He tried to break a hole in it but it held. He couldn't see a thing. He was forced to slow down and stop, otherwise they would end up hitting one of the gnarled trees on the roadside — or worse, an oncoming car. He came to a stop in a lay-by just over the dunes from the beach, stuck with a gun, a bag of meth and no bullets.

Stretch and cohort parked their bikes.

Stretch ran over and tore Matt from the driver's seat and dragged him deeper into the lay-by.

The red-haired guy grabbed BJ by the scruff of the neck and pulled him over the side of the ute. He tripped Matt's father, who fell on his face as he was trying to flee, but in the commotion Kristy jumped out of the truck on the road side and was gone into the night.

Matt dug his heel into Stretch's foot and elbowed him in the stomach. Stretch let go. The other guy with curly red hair and a Zapata moustache couldn't run to help or he would lose his grip on BJ and Matt's father. Stretch back-handed Matt who went down but recovered to his hands and knees. His father and BJ looked on in horror, powerless to release Ginger's hold. Out of desperation, BJ tried an elbow in the guy's guts but it missed its target, and Ginger gripped him even tighter.

"You're not so tough now, are you, surfer boy?" Stretch said and kicked him in the stomach. Matt doubled and fell.

"Come on … finish him off," said the ginger-haired one who held the others.

"Sure thing, bro," he said.

Matt stumbled to his feet. "Up your arse!" he shouted

in reply, and just as Stretch was about to lay a series of punches to Matt's head, Matt suddenly lunged towards him then stepped back and struck like a king cobra. "Take that, shithead!" It was a classic tae kwon do roundhouse kick to the head. Only one was required and Stretch's long lean frame dropped as if he had just suffered a serious wipeout from an unforgiving wave.

It was the same kick that had dropped Snake. Ginger had to either let his captives go to get Matt, or keep hold of them and let Matt get him. It was a no-win situation for him. Matt knew it would soon be all over. Ginger held tight. He must have decided it was a bird in the hand — in this case two birds — and he wasn't going to let go.

Matt took a length of four by two from the back of the ute. "Drop them," he snarled.

The guy let them go and charged Matt, swinging a right hook. Matt ducked and swung the length of timber at him, head height. There was a hollow thunk of wood hitting bone and down the guy went. He fell in a crumpled heap alongside the ute. They were free ...

Matt's whole body was light and his head spun, in a good way. He wondered where Kristy was, but he was sure she would be OK.

They left the bikers where they had fallen in the lay-by alongside the ute, complete with gun and meth waiting for the cops. They set off at a run to Matt's house, which was only a block away.

Kristy met them at the front door. "Don't worry, guys, I called the cops," she said, "but I kept any names out of it. As far as they are concerned I'm an anonymous passer-by."

She knew where Matt and his mum kept the key, under a pot plant on the back patio. From the lounge window, if they craned their necks, they could see it all. Kristy got changed into a pair of Matt's jeans and a hoodie. She gave the jacket back to Matt's father. It was a question of who would get to the abandoned ute first, the bikers or the cops. They didn't have long to wait. The cops got there a little quicker. They looked on as officers found the two beat-up bikers, and searched the vehicle. The night took on a hue of blue and red flashing lights.

Matt watched as a tall, thin officer in charge took something from the ute. He guessed a gun and half a kilo of meth. Snake arrived first with two sidekicks, and minutes later the rest of the Sidewinders drew up and stopped behind the ute. Soon the street was buzzing with squad cars and uniformed officers. Sykes and Wilson were among them. More police cars arrived as the cops radioed for backup. Traffic backed up.

Officers cuffed Snake and the rest of the bikers with hands behind their backs and shoved them into a paddy wagon and waiting cars. Matt, Kristy and BJ jumped up and down and cheered. The two casualties were stretchered into waiting ambulances. Matt's father stood erect, quiet but smiling. "You'd wonder why those idiots didn't hightail it when they saw the flashing lights. Snake must have known the meth was in there."

"He will just deny any knowledge of it or say it was planted. If the worst happens, that's what the prospects are for," Matt said. "He will just say it belongs to them."

"Yeah, he didn't have a law student for a girlfriend and learn nothing," said BJ.

"Well, I'm just glad we are free for now," Kristy said.

TWENTY-FIVE

MATT HEARD his mother's VW beetle come up the drive and the noisy motor cut out. The front door opened. "You home, Matt?" she shouted.

"Yeah, Mum! In the front room," he replied.

She clip-clopped along the hardwood floor into the lounge where he stood around the window with the others watching the commotion on Marine Parade. "Where have you been and what's happening over there?" she said.

"Some gang thing … we think, who knows?" It was better to keep her in the dark. It was a classic case of what she didn't know couldn't hurt her. Yeah, everything was cool the way it was.

"And why's Kristy dressed in your clothes?"

"She got wet at the beach." He had to admit that was a pretty good excuse, seeing they spent so much time in the water.

His mother put her hands on her hips and huffed. "Why didn't you let me know what you were doing?" Her eyes were wild. "I've had phone calls from BJ's and Kristy's parents — worried sick."

"I'm sorry, Mrs Avery," Kristy said. Her straggly blonde hair fell in her eyes.

"Me too," BJ said. His eyes were downcast.

"The surf was so good. We kept going till it was too dark. Then the Hilux broke down." Matt tried to be as convincing as he could. He was getting a bit worried. All this lying was coming a bit too easily. It was just that he wanted to save his mother from any heartbreak. She would never cope if any of her friends got wind of his drug dealing. It would destroy her.

"Why didn't you phone?"

'We got caught up in events," he said. "We didn't think." He couldn't tell her they were literally tied up, and Snake had taken their phones.

She turned to his father. "How'd you get here?"

"We bumped into them in Brighton. Trish dropped us off."

"Well, now we're all here, I'll make some coffee." She walked over to the kitchen and put the jug on and dug some biscuits out of the tin and placed them on a plate.

"Yum!" Matt said. He absolutely loved her hokey-pokey biscuits. He was so happy to be out of the Sidewinder's clutches, it made them taste even sweeter. But he would be happier if he hadn't put Kristy and BJ through it, and, he had to admit reluctantly, even his old man.

"I always liked your baking," his father called out, then sat down on the couch beside Kristy.

Matt sat in an armchair set at angles to the couch, but BJ stayed gazing out the window.

"Maybe we can breathe a sigh of relief now," his father said quietly.

His mother brought coffee and biscuits over on a tray and placed them on the coffee table. "Relief … about what?"

"Oh, just that the kids are back home from their ordeal at the beach."

She took the tray back to the kitchen then returned and sat on the couch. "Oh, I wondered what you were talking about."

"I could do with some relief," Kristy said. "I start uni next week. And I'm going to make my parents very happy. I've decided to go back to law after all, instead of teaching. So I can help put people like those filthy Sidewinders away for a long time."

"Good call," Matt said. He was fully aware that, even though the cops had arrested them, they were still a potential threat to them.

"I don't need convincing," his father said. "I think it is important to follow your heart."

His mother's mouth went wide momentarily. "Since when?"

"Since very recently," he said.

"I never thought I would see the day." She looked at him over the top of her glasses.

BJ butted in. "I'm going to finish drama school then get into the movies."

"Way to go," Matt said. It was good to see BJ was still passionate about acting.

"That's a laudable dream," his father said. "Our goals must be a dream first."

"Just a minute. That's what I've always said!" She nodded indignantly.

"I know. I'd stopped listening."

Matt gave his mother a knowing smile.

There was a knock on the door and his mother answered it. It was Mrs Jamieson. Her voice rang down the hallway.

"Is Kristy here?"

"I'm in here, Mum!" Kristy yelled from the lounge.

"Oh, thank goodness. We were worried sick. If we didn't find her here, Bob was going to call the police."

Matt thanked his lucky stars that Mr Jamieson hadn't come in. He always felt the atmosphere with Kristy's old man. He was sure he only accepted him for Kristy and her mother's sake.

Kristy got up to go; BJ and Matt followed her to the door.

"What are you doing in those strange clothes?" Mrs Jamieson said to Kristy.

"They got wet," she replied.

Mrs Jamieson turned to BJ. "We can drop you off on the way, if you like."

"Cool, Mrs J." BJ followed her out to the car.

Matt yelled at BJ's back as he went out the door, "Catch you for a surf tomorrow!" He and Kristy lingered in the hallway. He took her in his arms. "I love you," he said. He stroked and smelled her sun-bleached hair. His heart was heavy with regret and his face hot from embarrassment. "I'm so sorry about the shit I put you through." He stammered, "Can you ever forgive me?"

"Well …" Her mouth was tight and her eyes cloudy. "I'll have to see. You were, like, so stupid!"

It was a long time since poetry had moved him but a few lines teased at his brain. It was Shelley's *Love's Philosophy:* "*… And the sunlight clasps the earth,*

And the moonbeams kiss the sea —

What are all these kissings worth,

If thou kiss not me?"

In a flash her eyes sparkled and her lips pouted. "Come here," she said and drew him down into a long smouldering kiss. "Does that answer your question?"

"Let anyone try to keep us apart." They didn't need her old man's support — they loved each other, and that's what was important. He broke the clinch.

She replied from Coleridge's *Ancient Mariner:*

"*… A sadder and a wiser man,*

He rose the morrow morn."

Kristy headed out the front door to her father's car. Halfway there she turned around and said, "See you at the beach tomorrow."

"Sure. But I like to think … happier. I've given up shooting albatrosses!" he yelled back.

He shut the door behind her and went back to the lounge. Kristy's scent clung to his nostrils. All the drama with the Sidewinders hadn't rubbed that off. His mother and father were sitting on the couch. He sat down in an armchair.

"How's the surfboard business?" his father said. His grey eyes were intense.

How cool that his father was keeping his mother off the scent of what happened. It was decent of him. "Well … we now produce surfboards for international surf labels." His chest heaved with pride.

His mother's face glowed. "They are doing well."

"What's that mean in real terms?" his father said.

"Well," Matt said leaning forward in his chair, "we design, shape, do the artwork … and then export boards by the container-load to clients. They then supply them to their shops all around the world.

It's big business. Jack wants me to become an apprentice, eventually." His face glowed. His father would have to accept he was on the brink of an alternative career now.

"So you don't think you could have used an A+ in Economics?" his father said, cupping his hands together in his lap.

"Maybe … but Jack hires experts for that."

"And you don't want to be that expert."

"No. I'd much sooner create and shape."

"I can't say I blame you," his father said.

Matt lay back in his chair. He took in an extra deep breath and then exhaled.

"I wish we had this conversation a couple of months ago."

His father leaned forward. "True, it was a mistake. I'm sorry."

Well, that was something he didn't expect to hear from his old man. It called for a reply, and he wasn't sure if he was ready yet.

"And I'm sorry, too …for most of it."

He stretched his legs out in front of him. His mind drifted to all that had happened over the summer; it was unsettling. He worried about a backlash from the Sidewinders. But for the moment the family was closer than it had been for a long time, even before that fateful day when his father left. It was getting late and he had a big day's surfing with Kristy and BJ tomorrow. They would bury this whole sorry saga in the cleansing motion of the waves.

About the author

Leon Paulin grew up in Auckland and Dunedin, New Zealand. After leaving high school, he moved to Christchurch and hung out with a group of surfers around North New Brighton. He was soon riding the waves and soaking up the beach culture.

He worked in many manual jobs but later moved on to university. Eventually, he opened a string of used book stores and took up the pen.

His articles and short stories have appeared in newspapers, magazines and an online journal.

This is his first published novel.